WarFair4.com

Part One: The Day the-Market's Stood Still:

In a country well governed: poverty is something to be ashamed of.

In a country badly governed wealth is something to be ashamed of.

Confucius (551-479)

It has been said that love of money is the root of (many) evil(s) & a wandering from the path which has brought-upon us much pain: The lack (need) of money is so quite as truly:

Samuel Butler (1835-1902) EREWHON Ch: 20 (amended after: The Old Testament: 1Timothy: & Mark Twain (Mark Twain's Notebook 1909):

If the man & the woman bear their fair share of work: they have a right to their fair share of all that is produced by all: & that share is enough to secure them wellbeing: What we proclaim is The Right to Well-Being: Well-Being for All!

Pyotr Kropotkin (1842 –1921) The Conquest of Bread; Mutual Aid: A Factor of Evolution.

"The world has enough for everyone's needs but not enough for everyone's greed." Mahatma Gandhi (1869-1948)

To deny people their human rights is to challenge their very humanity –

Nelson Mandela (1918-2013)

"I have come this evening to talk with you on one of the greatest issues of our time - that is the preservation of human freedom: "

Eleanor Roosevelt The Struggle for Human Rights delivered 28 September 1948: Paris: France.

Tunisia 17th December 2010: According to friends & family: local police officers had allegedly targeted & mistreated Bouazizi for years: including during his childhood: regularly confiscating his small wheelbarrow of produce; but Bouazizi had no other way to make a living: He continued to work as a street vendor: Around10 p:m: on 16

December 2010: He had contracted approximately 450 dinarin debt to buy the produce: He was to sell the following day: On the morning of 17 December: he started his workday at 8 a:m: Just after10:30 a:m:: the police began harassing him again: ostensibly because he did -have a vendor's permit:

Bouazizi did -have the funds to bribe police officials to allow his street vending to continue: Bouazizi: angered by the confrontation: went to the governor's office to complain & to ask for his scales back: The governor refused to see or: listen to him: Bouazizi then acquired a can of gasoline from a nearby gas station & returned to the governor's office: While standing in the middle of traffic: he shouted: "How do you expect me to make a living?" He then doused himself with the gasoline & set himself alight with a match at11:30 a:m: local time: less than an hour after the altercation:

WF4.2.

Contents

WF4.4.

WarFair4: Rogue-Citizen: Global-Citizen:

Part One: The Day the Market's Stood Still:

1: She:

'It's like living in a rabbit hutch...'

She often said metaphorically & He replied with a shrug: *Nothing to say in reply: It was & it would take long enough to pay for: Eight-floors up: Looking over the street below now starting to become busy with traffic:*

They had lived with his parents for a time: & then after they were married: in a small rented flat: before they needed to afford somewhere to live together & to bring-up their two small children:

They had both saved: & with some financial help from a relative (deceased) they had managed to get this place: When the housing market was 'buoyant' & mortgages easy to get: The home was bought with a loan: a promissory note: deposited & co-lateraled together with the home it-self:

They were afloat: Both worked to pay-off the loan: which

although it was supposed to reduce each year did -seem ever to keep-up with pay & prices: The loan would anyway be paid-off many times over if they were ever to pay-off the debt: if this place was ever to become their own:

If they managed to keep paying-off the loan for the 'shelter from the storm' as they called it: That they did -now own: & were mortgage indebted to & may never actually own outright if they could -keep up with payments to be forced to sell-back sell-off at lower saleable price the difference between buying & selling-price which they would have lost completely: no recourse: & be homeless: or: back to parents & over-crowding: with friends similarly fixed; & their home: such as it was: re-possessed by the mortgage company:

A two-bedroom apartment: she thought of: *kitchen: lounge: shower-room toilet: & tiny balcony onto the world below: & between them & the sky above: Each month: & each successive year into the unthinkable future; two-thirds of two-lifetimes at least: Almost two-thirds every month of what they were both paid: She did the household accounts: & she knew: Of every week: every month: every year: every decade two thirds the home: the loan would have been paid for several times over by the time: if ever: it became theirs & theirs' their children's & perhaps even their Grand-childrens' one- day: But that is the nature of the human animal: is it not?*

To do over: & to be done over to: again & again? she thought; & in the quiet: mind wandering moment of pillared door: a room: a table: *a bed let go & a bed sheet left behind: ready to be buried with perhaps: as they did in the olden times: shrouded* as now by thin- curtains pulled-back:

Each worked to pay off the loan on the house & to pay for food & bills & extras: clothes: & nights out: occasionally: maybe twice a month: or: not-at all:

Then He had been laid off work at The **Bread&Cakes** *Bakery:*

Three-day-week: & three days wages:

The mortgage was re-negotiated: & they continued struggling to pay-off the loan & other loans: credited & debited from what they both now earned together:

There was never an issue of who should earn more & be the main breadwinner & who would do the most caring of each other: & the children: the unpaid responsibilities shared around the-home: &in: the-World: of-work&shopping&holidays with: other friends & family out-there similarly fixed:

They were equal: without even having to think about it: or: confront: N/n-wide societies & others' false expectations of gender & families: They were equal: & supported each other's frail & fragile egos with a natural equanimity: respectful & loving: each contributing their best & differently: to make the whole: It is -all doom & gloom she did often think: & he tried -to think on it:

The homely claustrophobia only had to be relieved by going out: To the cinema: to a bar or: restaurant: But that was - very often: Now that there were children as well: Seldom did extras make their mark: Clothes bought carefully a piece at a time: replacement rather than extra'vag®ance:

The cupboards filled with groceries: & emptied by the time the next weeks shopping is needed: & the next-weeks' earning's spent:

*

She was awake first this morning: & she got up from the bed on which he still lay awake but not-yet awake enough to leave its nigh-time warmth: She went through to the next room: The bedroom led across the narrow passage to the living room which led directly to the tiny gallery kitchen & balcony on one side & the door to the front room on the other:

Except it wasn't the front-room: exactly only like the 'front-room' of her childhood *playing on the street & door directly to the rugged matted smell of cooking from the stone wall white-washed country-kitchen:*

Upstairs two bedrooms: one on the gallery landing for the children: & a closet room to flush away with a basin of water from the kitchen sink: into the slurry sump: where you could hear it 'slurry' all the way down; & then back down to replace from the kitchen or: outside tap: pumped up from the well: refilling the fired earthenware clay bowl for washing: & zinc-metal bucket: ready for the next use:

At bedtime children first: then the adults: Rats' nested runs: beetles & cockroaches were kept away by the domesticated cats & dogs: horses at the local stables to ride at week-ends: & holidays: each week into the market town for food supplies: & children's treats:

Their whole world a living market place: work & play: now great enclosed parked superstores & supermarkets & factory outlet warehouse: Where goods are now transported: she *thought* of: *to & from: & by foot & h& carted & motor vehicle train tanker & container-ship from the docks & cargo-airport at the City-Harbour hub-humming away remote yet directing everyday life: everywhere:*

They with the affordable flight to get away from it all: necessary: a change: a necessary move: once-in-a-while: -every year but to visit family here & there & elsewhere: or: else you'd go stircrazy; do a night-time flit: leave the rent: the mortgage: un-paid: Only to otherwise to keep on fighting for the bargain:

WF4.9.

cheapest within budget: to get through the next day: & the day after that: When debts & fines could -be paid: the debt collector: buy-back take-back bailiffs: the selling-off of the personal possessions: & the debt: The laptop computer on sleep: & awakened: opened: placed on the table: booted-up & she texted instantaneously her thoughts: *We all need a roof over our heads & food put on the table:*

Without any other word or: contextual continuity that did remain obvious to everyone & anyone in the same & similar circumstances getting hold-of the hastily tapped-out short-message only excluding those without anything: home or: food: & those with patently far too much fire-walled or: pay-walled say whatever they *wanted*: & her *thought* continued in the context of the mindful moment *& that which we all must pay extortionately for over & again even when the food is eaten & the crap washed away there remains a nasty stain: a nasty taste: the original wages sweated over& the loans ever in negative-equity!*

Looking down now: not-in dejection but circum-spection:
(L)On(*e*)ly(e) but not for-long…

mechanised traffic building-up soon into a busy rush-hour congestion: Cars & buses: bicycles: motorbike: & motorised delivery truck: *from here: only another view:*

From two-sides: *from all sides now & the bedrooms along the corridor: along the passage the sleeping children slept earlier peeked into soundless in beautiful dream or: dreamless seeming startling worrying death-checked for breathing:* crossing from night into daytime TV: remotely automatically turned on: confirmation: that *life goes on:* The living room: as she entered bore all the chatter & the silence of one who listens: Still & safe: cosy & secure: The other rooms took over the emotions & needs: sleep & food: Love & arguments: The central room: the central chamber: looked on & awaited eventual: almost inevitable but never certain: reconciliation & rest: Indulged in social events: noisy chatter: & quiet evenings indoors: The furniture was adequate & filled the room: table: chairs: television: a drawer & shelved cabinet standing against a wall: displaying various icons: Family photographs in frames: a portrait of a film star: or: a print of a famous oil painting: ornaments: statuettes: figures of worship & of novelty: The furniture: the infrastructure: from the livelihoods: & eventually the roof over our heads *in over our heads* heard as if as originally spoken: There were opened envelopes & cajoling leaflet advertisement *Kill your debts! Die debts!* she thought of: circular-letters & bills for payment: propped up behind a ticking clock: There was a picture postcard from someone-else's holiday forming a picturesque frontage to hide the stack of demands for reply & payment which lay beyond: She drew back the curtains & looked out of the window across the

WF4.11.

balcony: with its unflowering plants growing in earthen clay flower-pots: It was still misty outside from the early morning warming; & she gazed over an area where many lived: & it seemed to her: this morning: where they too just lived out their lives: *day to day: week to week: They too thought to themselves that the world must have always been this way* as she looked-out onto the dawn of a gradually opening *new*-day:

WF4.13.

2: They:

They had stayed together & with two little ones: one of each: girl: & boy: by the time they're both about to be in school: they could -risk another to bring up: & the cost of it: They only hoped they would hold on to their jobs: & worked hard: Difficult hours: & some days-off: Where the rotas work-out for childcare: family: or: neighbours: parents now friends of the children's friends who lived conveniently nearby: the social network from the cradle to school:

They had met when things were starting to get a bit tight: get difficult again: for most: school-meals free often without a meal some-days meaning: the situation for most working families: for those looking-for work & those in-work things had -got any better: ||/or any: easier really during the so-called good-times & both parents were needed to work to keep the family going:

Voluntary social networks became all the more significant & reciprocal: Shared- care with child & adult interaction social & meaningful: shared-lives:

They had both kept their jobs in more or: less 'essential services' although -without their job-cuts: never-the-less: When: (nn/nn/nnnn... *nn/nn/nnnn) running...*

WF4.14.

The Bakery factory went on three-days week&pay to-match: he had more time to be with the children & help with others' children familiyies' and friends still in fulltime work: her awkward-hours shiftwork...

He had done some building work on the odd-days: to fill-in: She'd done some shop-work & garment-making before: all the Shop- Jobs: 'Retail': were filled: & not-hiring: They had moved to his folks in The City: suburbs really: inner-urban: something-like-that:

His mother had worked at The Mill & got her a job there: & then him working at The **Bread&Cakes** *Factory where familiyies on the past had delivered milled grain-flour: at the top of the road: when they had moved-in together & had kids: His father's family had been itinerant-millers: before that: gypsies: travellers village town to village town: They did well: Moving around (funnily enough* she thought *like business-people nowadays do: by road to visits salespeople in the retail outlets: home-shops and in other words: Super-Markets: Big-Business: They by aero'plane to meetings here there & everywhere:*

Cities all-over to do deals on a massive global-scale: now worth billions of whatever the currency: sometimes dealing even the currency itself: In the past when the work dried-up they moved 'moved along' or: stayed & waited for more or: different labour:

Out of work: they always found something: When the gig-

work was finished: they moved-on: along the waterways: they had a farm in the countryside for a while & the parents still lived there:

They then through the Industrial Future:

The Soul of The City:

Across The-River bridge across the tram tracks: & by the railway station: The Heart of the City: the Financial Quarter: Settling: they self-employed: their-own bosses...

Hers' She-thought-of: employed: not-their own boss: On some land: Renting: Then they eventually: moving taking-out a home-loan buying: homeowners now: investors in their own future&their childrens' childrens'...

*

Soon the television was blaring as usual in the morning in the main room: that was empty for the moment: & beyond where she was now dressing hurriedly: & he was brushing his hair frantically:

There was the noise of children getting washed & dressed: with incessant commentary & conversation to each other: & any other: or: just to themselves: To each other: a one-way argument: older to younger incited over some triviality: shouted back in frustration: at that point the only-game-in-town & to be fought-out until one of them is crying & the other shouting-the-odds; before calm is brought: *evens* by one or: other parent: supervising: supposedly: to the other at least while they all got ready for work: school & preschool nursery: The sound of the kettle screaming on the kitchen cooker; & television advertisements conveying to deaf ears: & blind eyes: but perhaps receptive memory:

'The Best in the World':

Or:

'Longer-lasting…' or: whatever the dubious rarely unique selling-point *perhaps to be unconsciously recalled later that day at the supermarket:*

At present they seemed to be of no avail: Both rushed-to: get the children to school: & themselves out-to: work: To earn the pay that would pay the prices at the supermarket later that day:

'Where is my shirt?' he

called:

'Where you last put it!' she retorted as she entered the living room she found her shoes under a chair: & stopped-in front of the television: The networked advertisements ended: & the programme returned to the main story of the day:

'There is no money to pay share dividends: or: to buy shares with:' he flicked the remote control onto an-other channel &got:

'Individual & group share prices have collapsed; or: become so high that they have become worthless: Confidence has collapsed: debt undiminished: Price increases have been blamed: Increases in pay&pensions have been blamed:

Increases in interest-rates & profit-levels have been blamed: Each of these has pushed share prices ever upwards:

As share prices & shop prices overtake the customers' ability to pay & the ability to pay pushes these prices down: profit margins recaptured by increases in interest rates & prices: have pushed share prices up even further:'

& a-view passed across the screen to locked factory-gates: ports& land-sea borders closed to traffic or: trade:

It *did not-seem too bad: or: even unusual: the television experts & announcers liked to make a big deal out of anything* she thought: *It was their jobs after all:*

The pictures shifted-to: City office-buildings: that only a few were being allowed into: & then to the becoming crowded squares & circuses around Town & City centres all over the globe:

all the streets & roads & highways leading there; the TV reporter turned away from the camera: & *let the scene* somewhere else: could be anywhere: *speak for itself*:

In the kitchen radio reports followed from the stock-markets around the world:

'Tokyo Nikkei: Shanghai: Hang Seng Hong Kong:

Bangkok: Delhi: RTS Moscow: Frankfurt: Cape Town: London & Canada stock Exchanges: New York Wall Street Buenos Aires & Rio…' as she went to look for tea-bags he got the cups out & put some bread under the grill to toast:

As the cups were emptied & the door was opened to go out the stock-market reports were interrupted by the radio-announcer:

'We: have heard in the last few minutes that: The International Conference of the Leaders of Governments & World Banks meeting in Geneva: are to make statements at midday mean-time on the current state of financial affairs across the globe:

'The Economic-Crisis' around *the*-World...'

They stopped & looked at each other as they heard the announcement:

'What will they come up with this time I wonder?' she asked aloud: to him: & to the radio speaker: & as she went to the bathroom door:

'Come on you two!' to the children: & to him in the-

same: breath:

'What time are you finishing today?'

'On-Lates' his reply; with a shrug: noticed: as she said:

'I'll have to clock off early then' & she thought: *another opportunity to sack me: but if school finishes before work what are we supposed to do?*

'I'm taking them in: anyway!' he called:

'I know!' she replied:

'We will have to go to the supermarket tonight:' added knowingly & *a reluctant necessity when it came to it*:

'Or tomorrow anyway:' as he kissed her quickly on the lips: quickly quietly tantalisingly: knowing this weekly & often daily shopping-trip is what they did all this for:

Along with the mortgage-rent&love of their familyies'& children: smiling: He went out of the door onto the communal hallway:

'Another financial crisis!' he called out: with more than a note- of: sarcasm: which did -need any reply other than a disinterested:

'Is there?'

WF4.20.

She went back inside the living room & went to turn the television off: as the announcement of the impending declaration from government leaders & world banks was being repeated:

'Won't make any difference!' she shouted over the noise of the television:

'…never does!'

& she left the house soon afterwards:

WF4.21.

3: He:

He took the stairs with the children: two-at-a-time one in a pushchair: the other just learning to walk: & they headed off together for The **Food&Drink** corner-shop: turning the top of the road pushing the baby buggy uphill: the almost unmade sidewalk pavement now in disrepair: showing the lack of maintenance through the good times as well as the now financial re-cession:

Telling *the- walker*: as He&She said to each other in jest *the- children laughed at that:* but the one no-longer holding on to the buggy: called-out to: The-Other:/||:

'Hold on to the buggy' answering the constant questions:

'What is this?' & 'What is that?' & having to say:

'Be careful!' every two-minutes: &:

'Stop! making me have to say:

'Be Careful' every two-minutes!' & they giggling together: at what: he knew not-what:

Not even imagining a time when he & she would -be going to work: & they to school & nursery: then keeping them *in-to: ourdotage!*

WF4.22.

Going-to to pick-up the fallen one the other-one walking then the running-off child & he picking-up continuing walking:

'Don't Run!'

The *walking*-child only hearing the last word as *usual*:

'Run:'

& wondering what all the shouting was about: &:

'Stop at the corner!' hearing all the words this time:

'Alright!' *thoughtfully*:

'O.K!' trying out these new words heard from them & at school:

'Stop!' & stopping in the middle of the pedestrian pavement: to get collided in to & rolling on the ground giggling: getting-up&*running*-off: *laughing*: looking: : backwards:

'STOP!' at the corner of their road:
turning into the next:

'Stop: at the kerb!' He catching up: pushing the pushchair ahead: the walker hanging on: over the kerb & into the road: Looking both ways: & then both ways again: Then back again: one last way this time: *too- quickly…going*
to: Run!

WF4.23.

The way the traffic was headed: moving-faster<>*slowly*: one-car stopped: & let them across to a wave re-turned: w*atching-out: for all three* of them & to the oncoming traffic split by traffic lights commanding:

Stop Start or: Wait…watch…*pause*...

To the other side of the road safely to the other kerb: chasing on ahead to The-Shop: The 'little-one' in the buggy trying to get out to follow: shouting: & pointing with one: then both index-fingers: toward the road:

'Taxi!' swivelling around almost falling-out:

Pointing: ahead:

'Bus!'

The other returning: giggling:

'A: Bus!' correcting: & then at they passed the shop pleading verbally & non- verbally: tugging & whining for sugary *sweet*-sweet(s):

'Helicopter!' singing: & pointing & swivelling around

again:

'The **Food&Drink** Shop!' the other:

'Sweets! categorically:

WF4.24.

(U)(s)(u)-ally not-until they came home from school & nurs(e)ry(*e*):

Even then only some days: & if they had been: T/t: >?: good-at school or: nursery: but(T) all-ways worth a try:

Pointing: jumping up-&-down: out of the buggy: falling out: buckles unbuckled: by(*e*) *the-older-one*:

'As long as you behave yourselves today: & they're not-too bad for your teeth: & you clean your teeth!' *they knew that*:

Giggling all the more: at some reference only they knew: the words: the noises: & the tone of voice: the bedtime:

'Clean your teeth! Properly!!' the older one repeated: & they went into more fits of giggles: in-to: *the*-**Food&Drink** news' agent-grocers&con.fectionar(y)(L)ie(s)…' &/at: some-*time*: li-*censed* off-licence:

Where he: or: she: & they stopped each morning for a newspaper on the way to nursery: & school *when it was his-turn*:

As they crashed through the door the older one getting deliberately or: soit s(e(a)(emed: in the way of the baby-buggy: asserting rights over the other smaller & weaker; & not-unusually but always predictably in the morning *rush*-hours: *with: so many other things to think about:* the only thought: unable to think about anything else: *shopping*:

WF4.25.

The buggy *almost* tipped over in the raucous rumpus: the Older-One falling over the younger-one: strapped-in: straining at the straps: Letting out an ear-piercing yell: the older one still giggling until the younger lashed-out as only younger siblings know how too; & the older one let out a:

'Yell!' then a:

'Scream!' & apparently exaggerated explication of pain: &:

'Unfairness!'

'Come-on you're the older one: you should know better! Do you have to have to argue&fight over everything! No sweets!': & then he knew: as soon as he said that: that he was A Beaten Man:

A yet louder exclamation set up: While the younger-one looking on in glee: quieted & puzzled: twisted turned looking upwards to The Father; for some resolution to the questioning plea & fell out of the buggy: unbuckled:

'Me a' well?':

Looking up from the floor: the older standing-up & going to stamp on the younger: smiling sweetly now: the other sprawled on the floor: as-if: felled:

'The smiling assassin!' he called-out from the front of the shop in reference to the older child: & to The Shopkeeper who was stacking shelves from remaining stock: He: holding-up the regular National Newspaper: the shopkeeper called:

'You may as well keep that' to the loose change

being handed over the counter:-:

'…it will be like one of those free ones!'

'One of those comeback to byt(*e*)coins?'

'Not…'

Hearing:-listened to until afterwards: scanning the headlines the money left on the shop-counter: chuckling when the remark realised:

'No: I got it!' *minding The Children who were not-*

fighting: or: pretending to steal sweets: not-knowing any better

yet: yet knowing better: laughing & looking obvious:

The Shop-keeper bagged & handed-over what it was they wanted-most-of:

'There you are: for later…' the customary sweets as a gift now *in-change sometimes anyway: for a small note passed across the counter:* From the Shopkeeper to them…& then to-him:

'Daddy keep-it: for later' the children looking pleased: & anxious also: that they might have to 'keep it for later' & only then the conditional:

'…& only if you are good today!'

Given to the Father: patiently waiting to get off to nursery: school: & work: Again consternation: put-on: by the older child: to the younger: *pouting*: dropped lower-lip: Acting-out: pretending: face pulling: Puzzled at: & copied by the younger: Both laughing at this: & between themselves: at something they did not-really know what it was *to be good* or: *all day*; or: even how to attain: *this*:

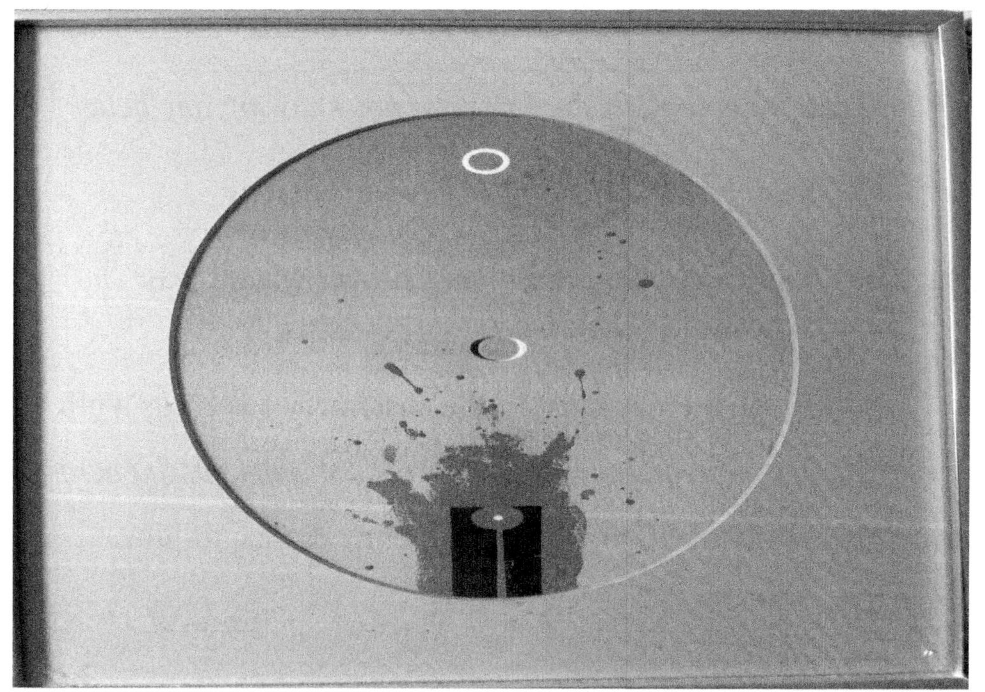

WF4.28.

4: The Accident&Emergency:

She had pressed the OFF switch: & they all had left for school & work closing all the windows & door behind her a short while later & going where others' had left: or: were still leaving front doors for the days school & work: & activity ahead:

Outside & downstairs: through the piles of discarded

rubbish&the-door wedged open: To the blocked refuse-chute: to the stairs & the *If-it's-working* lift down to the ground floor: t*he worst thing standing inside the open lift door: -being sure if the elevator was going to work: or: not:*

Or go crashing to the ground: like everything else:

This day she was *on-a-late* & so *he was taking the children to school & nursery: he would be collecting them later today* it seemed *when his shift finished later that day:*

She entered the same shop that he with the children had left a few minutes earlier:

'Got any bread in?'

'You may as well take one there: only one-day-stale!' climbing-down off a stool-from-stacking-shelves:

'It's gone stale already: hasn't it?' continuing:

'Never mind the bakery! Haven't seen them yet today...'

Today the shop was open as usual: ready to stock-up again with the usual days-supplies that had been 'phoned in the day before: or: other-wise: relatively:

'It looks like it is: whenever the Delivery-Van turn(s…)

up!'

If/Then: &/or:

'Your other-half works at The-Bakery doesn't he?'

'He's taking the children-to: school…'

'My-other went out early *enough* today-to: hunt-*catch:* The Cash&Carry & not-back yet! I phoned-in the order: They said nothing's moving yet: still there I expect…they're *still*: in the queue…'

Now: pointing at the dry loaves on the shelf:

'Going.. stale!' momentarily paused: then:

'No Cash: No Carry!' exclaimed:

'Fresh is best!' The Shopkeeper continued to her:

'Cost&Con.venience: sugar salt additives addictive fatty-

acid pre-servatives ultra-processed packaged for quick-*profit(s')*

take-away. Throwaway! *Fizzy* drinks cans&bottles snacks&

sweets wrappers…you name it! This we get from your bakery: you know: it doesn't last…'

'Not *my*-bakery…' she uttered & the shop-keeper unheard or: mis(s)-heard con.t(i)nu(*i*)ng:…

'I have-to buy on credit & then it gets chucked anyway unsold! I have to *Health & Safety* it I give it to *The Bin-Raiders* out the back: they have it!' continuing:

'Still: can't blame them can you? Poor beggars: Families some of them homes as well I leave it for those that take it: homeless: you know: or: out of work on our taxes' Social-Benefits that go nowhere: they stay poor & hungry & homeless: They take it home: or: toast it on one of those outdoors braziers they sleep under the bridge arches: you know? Don't seem to worry them! All yesterday's bread has gone: Only one left now: we won't get another delivery today I dare say & I am told we don't know when! Only the newspapers: so far: delivered & I haven't paid for them yet: Don't get payback for what I don't sell…cash up-front credit/debt always…'

'How is that!!' she doubly surprised at the apparent revelation: that *everything had to be paid-for up-front & prior to any sales in lieu of any sales & lost if -sold forced to sell or: giveaway at any cost always selling pitching the product off the shelves…*

The shopkeeper arrived from the back of the home-shop where their cramped family quarters were called home & once more into the shop towards the counter: & continued:

'You can give me all the money you've got if you like: No cash for change though: cheap sweets instead: like the last time! The Banks are not-open: so you won't be able to get any Government notes or: cash out anyway: Never be able to sell this place now: You know: I've been trying to sell-off? The Shop & its stock: to pay off loans & bills on the shop & on the stock; but no buyers…'

'Not-yet?'

'Not-now: I'd have to sell-off at even more of a too low a-cost: maybe we'll just up-&-go sometime: leave it all behind.'

'No buyers yet?' she asked: not-listening: heard it before; *& not-just this shopkeeper try as they will to stay afloat…for the price of* ***Bread&Cakes****!*

All the local shops were known: either by the name on the front of the shop or: the birth-nationality of the family that owned or: rented that shop & did their business there:

Small re-tailers she thought of *Family run businesses across the globe: despite the Supermalls & Hypermarkets still the way most trade finishes up: from the roadside stall to & from The Town & City marketplaces & streets of small shops...&: of course: the Stock-Markets & Money-Markets...they pay ahead & fix the prices there & then*...she pondered...like the bread the news lasts one-day then the next...

She looked at the front page of the newspaper un-folded & thrown onto the worn light dark varnished & metal-trimmed wood surface: glanced at a cartoon which depicted the worlds finance ministers: heads in h& s: sitting on stacks of money: no words needed: but a comment she read for free without intending to buy: turning-over onto the inside page:

In the last weeks & months there have been queues

in: shops for scarce goods rationed by ability to pay:

There have been queues to spend money instead of

saving-by *investing*-in...

*Home: stocked&shared in-surance pensions&personalnot-for personal profits penned: familyies' profit in happiness routea©ting-out of least-*pain *least resistance before self&other becoming worthless inflated beyond affordable value:*

The prices of goods & services have increased week by week & day by day: as more… *don't we just know it!*

So what's so different! she pondered again:

She wondered: *how the small shops & retailers & service providers like health & social care: whether cottage hospitals or: fast-food how they managed at all with all the out-of-town Shopping-Malls&Giant Chain-Stores that everyone shopped at because they could afford the prices & special offers:*

The supermarkets paid upfront: but cheaply & only what they thought they could sell at a good profit: & what: people could afford...

The-Shopkeeper had continued without stopping stocking the shelves along the aisleway finished:

'…that's it! Everything is out: I'm now officially out of stock!' thought: *apart from what I've got in the back for me & the family for a few days: & that's it!* the train of thought returning to re-stacking the shelves with the meagre remaining stock: &/with: *some(N/n...* fin.ali(t)(y/n): 1.0...

'Not stock-piling not-getting in even enough buying customers to cover the existing loans on capital: Stock&Shop rent is unpaid for the year...'

Back at the counter: handing the money-back:

'You may as well take it! Here: why don't your other-half bring us some nice freshly baked bread to stock up the shop with? That is where he works isn't it? They've closed the works again: did you know? I owe them anyway: The Bakery: The **Cash&Carry**: you name it! I'm well into negative-equity now: The amount the shop owes: never sell-up now: I will have to give-it away! Do a moonlight: That is where he works 'though: isn't it?'

'Not any more it seems...'

her sullen answer:

'How about a free newspaper! Everything else has been taken from us: they've bled us dry!!' exclaimed The-Shopkeeper: without irony restrained & mixed with an anxious *mirth*:

She said: to stem the apparent paradoxical merriment:

'You know we can't even get bread from the bakery he work-sat.:.*they* are that tight with their profits! *We* must buy it from the shops like every-one else even 'though he works there!'

she added:

'How stupid is that? Uncaring for your staff your workers…'

'The Bakery wants to make as much profit out of *us* as-they: can:.:'

'Out of all of us! Small shop-keepers & customers alike!'

'Never mind the measly pay! Anyway…'

pointing-a-thumb back through the door:

'If the works are: *closed*. no-bread:'

'& no-cakes either today:'

'Let them eat bread!' & the money for a small loaf was put on the counter & the small sliced loaf: in its mould-inducing plastic wrapper: & the newspaper with its banner headline declaring:

STOCK MARKETS IN CHAOS

was carried off:

-Will you be going into the rally?' texted when she had left the shop: & called his cell mobile-telephone with photograph&stored number: linked-in without answer or: voice-message checked: he texted immediately back:

-No point going in beforehand: I'll not-be getting…paid *anyway*…

5: The Banker & The Clerk:

The *investment* merchant-Banker sat-back: & glanced across at the *administrative* accounts:'-Clerk: sat in the opposite seat: fixed-table between: Travelling on this same-train same-time: same-carriage: - : For the-Clerk the *same*-seat: if that or: any other was to be had amongst the everyday commuters seated & a few standing-room only: today: Not/or: as today usually crammed-in each weekday: early-morning: into the City: For the-Banker: this day too-early for the usual…reservation with: or: today without waiter-served breakfast or: a free-morning newspaper:

On(e)ly those 'papers freely given-away & piled-up in the station forecourt to be taken-away: That had to be paid-for anyway by publicising the latest model & version: & most *reasonably*-priced:-like copies of The Big Issue sold-on: by homeless-people: in Metropolis' around the world: *no such thing as a free-lunch* the-Banker reasoned:

In First-Class The-Financial Newspaper: paid-for anyway by The Railway Company ticket-seated & breakfasted with The: *Financial-Newspaper* at massively *discounted* market-rate or:

cost-price *freely* as advertising encouraging in-someway paid-for & for: *returns*: *the*-newspaper could be easily afforded: anyway: Today's loss-leader every tomorrows' daily winner paid-for upfront at the station kiosk the-newspapers' corporate-investment credit/debt *knowingly borrowed on perma-credit: staff-costs paid-off monthly in lieu of-arrears paper-money metal in the bank cashed-in on continuing steady-sales to be recouped: shorted & long-term investment daily achieved...*

Today: the newspaper not-given-away with the extortionately: & exclusively permissive over-priced pass this day into the City' Stock-Exchanges & Financial-Markets:

The Annual-Executive rail-ticket paid-for: whether used or: not-*this* day the first train out & apparently only Standard-Class available:

A single First-class carriage was filled-up quickly by anyone who had a ticket & *conceivably some who did-not:* there were no-tickets being checked: or: paid-for *apparently the barriers left-open* & inviting *all-comers:*

For the-Banker: for another-time that morning: something mildly: now-seconded: & *markedly* un-usual:

The earlier: when the radio alarm-clock had switched-on routinely: with the early-morning fishing: farming: road: & rail conditions Airline & shipping delays: arrivals: & departures: & speculative *forecasts* weather-reports: from around the world:

Local: & global: political-economic & media-news: with the previous nights' *closing*...market-prices: *list*:...

There had been developments: overnight: that needed attending-to:

From the emptying platform: the-Banker & the-Clerk boarded the train together more or: less equal: The-Clerk with a free newspaper: & headphones plugged-in to a mobile Media-Centre: The-Banker for the first time in a long-while with a bought-copy of The *Financial-Newspaper* from the trains' limit-ed. refreshments'-trolley:

Having taken the first seat available in the nearest St&'ard-Class compartment coupled with a foul-stench reeking drain-leaking latrine *literally* retching: between the brown & grey-green patterned seats: along the narrow aisleway the-Banker waving the newspaper ahead *as if to clear-the-air*:

Un-wavering: when shunted across by the next-passenger inline to the only *vacant* window-seat glanced across-to & sedentarily leaned-forward across the table between them: & asked of the-Clerk already sat down-opposite:

'So: what do you make of it all then?' in the customary easy clear voice of one born with the interrogative confidence of swift appraisal:

As instantly as if mysteriously-*accusatory*…as if with some felt need for validation: valediction: justification: testimony: guilt? Even before any evidential fact: or: *fiction*?

With a self & another-deceiving finality: justifying: with instant-conviction: promised but of who? By whom? Despite the or:iginal opening-question: it seemed as if with no real right-of reply: The initial conversational-question asked as if not-*intended* to be replied-to or: any other-mindedly *mitigate(e)ing* circumstances or: any-answer-at-all particularly: or: generally listened-to:

Or so the younger-Clerk: surprised to be spoken-to then considered: *perhaps like a nurture-nature kind of thing? Possibly a Plebeian enquiry? Selected-standard flagged with no-probation* the-Clerk decided: *more likely a command: to make*

something of IT: to-be-taken-notice-of:

Notice-anyway given-of: dis-regarding the-possibly probabilityies' paranoid-maniacal rhetorical-answer awaited or: not: by either: or: Both: Regardless of the-Other*: The subtler -Inquisitor? The Quickest to-the- Draw?*

The original-*recipient* by-assumption looking-up from a streaming mobile smart-phone camera & video-games' console:

USB-4slot-machine:game:*downloading…*

PER (personal electronic reader)/de-pocketed-*information*recorded singularly removing the ear-phone microphone-socketedlead off-line *searching*: for the source of the *mildly-irritating openly questive-words' spoken* as directly-to: or: so it seemed to the-Clerk: in almost immediate reply:

'Senseless:' As to The-Banker as to the newspaper headline shaken-out: the whole carriage could now view:

The-Banker sat-back purposefully: purportedly: & provocatively: to:> unfold *The Financial-Newspaper* with the headline outer-most: upper-most:

WORLD MARKETS IN TURMOIL!

& *seen* again that photograph taking up the whole of the rest of the G*rey*-top printed front-page remaindered remained pictured in the *mind*s' eye:

Now: turned inside-out: & with a staring squeezed blink of the eyes: fumbled as if in a freak storm: a blown umbrella: folded quickly-away: To the-Clerk: hung-out to dry: having seen earlier the front-page photograph: & one-liner top headed:

WORLD MARKETS IN TURMOIL!

re-conceived on-line re-*connected*: down-loaded: & updating second to second milli-second: minute-to-minute *mobile-version uploading* freely with-advertising: optional: *Freeview* choice or: fee: *skipping*…the-Clerk looking-down & into the same recently concealed picture & slowly re-storing from *browsing*-history as accurately *acutely*-historically as-depicted as veritably verifying verifyabilityies' tapped un-tampered with-mobile: cell battery-phone photographed syndicated & World-Wide-Web: *network*ed-scene:

As at the end of the previous day: the-City: corporate-stocks & government-bond markets' as then as now: seen *news*-printed & pictured from the evening before: a *litter*-stream strewn like old ticker-tape: across the Trading-room floor forsaken & an *un-forgiving* blankly waiting-screen: strap-line banded:

Markets closed.

The single-slogan as about to go up or: down was not-possible to tell: Diagonally: from one corner of the screen to the other perhaps *tangentially*-to slip-backwards: smoothly-across continuously stuttering across perhaps only-slightly *blurred* from the-top aloft above: or: below: the perfect: the-*normal* midway *ideally*-positioned not-at the-*extreme* outer-fielded or: even ever truly-*centred:* but as *inside-out*&now: as stilled:

As then: as now: as no-longer not-equal=not-identical: existent: or: again: but: now: & then: anymore: *nowhere* at all: Except: now: there: only as stop-framed cinematographically stilled: to be recorded: & repeated: any movement as any-moment only *impendent*: in the-*cloud*: that bold bl& statement *flickering* nonetheless-memory *fuzzily* held in-abeyance:

Markets closed.

shimmering-pixelated grid-table mapping diagrammatic…a *flickering*…a coming-together: as a dawn held rising: over the Worlds'-Edge(s)=0

As a vertiginous horizontally remote-geometrically buildingsited:

Cityscape *skyline*: *diverting*-<u>Bank</u>ing-*details*: scam-scanning un-declared bribery&corruption: & fraud: on-consultancy & management-only contracts' hostaged-to: hi-jacking debt-ransoming deals: on: projected *un-founded* optimism &/or: pessimistically threateningly un-throated &/or: keeping-quiet: bailing-out from the*public* purse & then tax-dodging as if *this* would be enough to boostconfidence on-fixed & violin-*fiddling* figurative tree-*burning*: on-

paper:

WF4.43.

online screen date&time revealed:

<T1-T2: Strengths & Weaknesses: *sub-titling* screen-fantasy theme: *distinctive* emblematic-corporate-creations: *dis*-owning any *real*-identity &/or: real-*personality*: patched-together bufferzone: video-text typeset: *cast*-role freely-played-*ambiguous*ly between good & bad: between one-*price* & another up<up<up & down>x3 *in-correctly* dis-honestly &/v: x/y/z right-left uppityies'-down@ irrespons(ed.)ibl(*e*)y: sealing-the-deal:

Generic-key: *designer*-rip-off: online:
D*ialogue: open*-options: with-structure & *series* arcade-style *deviation* from the normal: *too* complex-to-control: if at all: *cutting*edge:

'Perhaps: bringing the-City down?'

'The-*Country*!'

'The-City: is: The-Country:'

'Being brought-down?'

'Scary': *the-World thus: Ethno-linguistically gender & ability driven:*

'Pluto-cracy…' *owned…*

'Down with the-Oligarchyies!' dis-

owned…

'Rapocracyies' strangled strategic-*falsely* promoted tactics…'

'Kleptocracyies'…'

'*Necrocratic* Bad-tactics…'

'What?'

'Barbarous State-of-Nature…'

'Dead-Civilisations'…'

'What?'

'Brought-down? Bought-out. Burnt-out. Destroyed…'

'By? Who? Why?'

'Grotesque *over*-investment in commercial-property leisure-luxuries funded by in-comprehensible:' (G)reed: grid-algorithm: *debt*-instrume(a)nts…

'Of: Tort-ur(e)! Succession!!!'

WF4.45.

< City-Investment Banker-Governments' local-decisions making-out at *each*-step each-player arriving as glob-ally neo-neat optimal-solution *good-better:* best at a-time T1-T2…

> T3 worse-worstshortingtime: with-out considering long-term consequentials'…

future: *im(p)act*:

Con.-sequentially sequential-appearing to be most-beneficial not-backtracking once-the: <> :decision is made binary:partners to: poly-nomial customers coded-in at-least conditionalityies' acceptabilityies'-noted:

nodal(i)ty(*i*)es'…<

<Economic-Efficient-Effectively(e) not-guaranteeing warrantee applic.abilityies' dependent-on: specific-a(i)lityies'…>

>Algorithms' combinatorials' attempting all-search at-once:
greedyies' exhaustive-exploration non-intellectual fathomingfunction(s): examined all-possibilityies' executing depleting distance-depleted discovery to one-single solution true/false/indifference engineering: good/bad/evil enforcing back-tracking all- options possible/practical trial-&-error plausible partial-valid *therefore* non-valid solution(s)…<

<Here&Now?

>The-Peoples' ourselves…

WF4.46.

<Big-Business! Core-Corp-oration(s)' Bank(s)': *list:...*'

'Brute-Force! Perhaps the-Price of Civilisation(s)'...'

'Growth-factoring…in: The Price of-Money! Big-Money!!!'

'Too-quickly?'

'Too-slowly:'

'Or -at all Now:'

'Bringing in the goods…'

'Not: bringing in the-goods…'

'Same as it's ever been. Bringing in the-Harvest: Or not: heated-markets…'

'T/r-o(l/l)(p/f)asting…'

'On-Fire! Drought-Famine Flash-Flood Global failure:'

'Weaponised decl(*e*)aring price-war-*hiked*:'

'<u>Trade-War</u>: *Tarriff*-on: raw-materials' produc(t1)ing…'

'Buy-low! (t2) Sell-high! (t3)…'

'*Live*-War…'

WF4.47.

'Vile-Raw Evil…'

declared privatee(ha!)-ring piracyies' global-banditryies'

'War on Want:'

'War is Want:'

'Global-failure:'

'Of the-*Banking*-System…'

'Utilities' Food&Medicines sanction-rationed against starv(e)at-ion…'

'Health…'

'Clean air&water…'

'Poisoning Pharming-systematic…'

'Gen.(un-et(h)ic-ally modification forced fixed sales prices…'

'Annual-seasonal planned-Farming:…'

'Coal Gas&Oil…this-*time*:…'

'Tech. Double-Bubble: money-bubbles' troublings'…'

'The Great North-Sea! saw Nothing like this!'

WF4.48.

'See.'

'Sore?'

'Saw?'

'Holy-See: across Seas Oceans & Land & more be-sides:...'

'Existence: In: Solar-Space & more besides...'

'Moon&Mars! Siezed! Solar-Wind Water-Farming Media-Tech: bonus on-top of: that! Nuclear! Energy-Waste Debt-Bailout printing-money paying no-Taxes:

'Who pays Taxes: in their right-mind?'

'Those who can get away with 'IT':

Libertarian Libertine-Liberal: Free-Trading: with the-Peoples' investment-futures' pensions' social-want(s): in-surance...

'In corpo'rating Pure-Profit! *non*-Tax Class! Corporate-Elite!!! Anti! Socially-secured shareholder pay-out prosperityies' properties' working-hard: play-hard!'

'Equityies'...'

'Equi-vocal?'

'Entityies'…

L/O(w)n(e)ly Nationalised: Presidential-CEO…'

'Public-Ownership?'

'Revenue? If you're the-Revenue: I don't *owe*:'

'No-return: no-comeback then?'

'Corporate Research&Design innovate: Cash-flow: Growth

de-flation base-rates' price-pay cost-of-work…' *platform sub.s…New-Money vs: Old-Money:*

Gross-Sales less-costs labour-calculated to avoid taxes simple! WellEarned! clean-living well fair fare trickle-down tax evasion charityies' well-spent cheated poisoned-chalice well…

fanfare-for: fair-shares to&from:…

0nline: on: @anymo-me(a)nt:

The same now: as far as either of them or: anyone on the train there:

WF4.50.

or: anywhere-else knew: as of the business dealings that evening before:

Both now in the knowledge assumed of the other: Both: assuming unknowingly yet simply *pictorially*- imagining that morning the scene as unchanged from the night before:

Then: as now: inside the City Stock-Market building heavy-teakwood mahogany door's: tightly-closed: hermetically-sealed: A normally *fluorescent* glow turned-off: Except for a single computer-screen presence remaining-there:

Markets closed:

as if readied for all time previous: for this day:

As if never happened before; yet it had:

Before the evening before: as in pointless pointed *dire*-warning: once installed: rightly or: wrongly even indifferently as if permanently equivocally librant perhaps automatically not-to be taken too-literally or: in-definitely: *normally* meaning: *before the cleaners had cleaned-up: & some: but then: not-everyone-else had been cleanedout* before *nightlife* restaurant & television cabaret: the latest news:

& re-pose: taken:

The: *on*-message only that:

'The-Markets will be open again & sooner *rather*-than:

later…' hearing the blessed-words:

'Sell! Sell! Sell!'

with:

'Buy! Buy! Buy!'

with nothing in-between

no-productivity no-caring

for: process-only…

speculation hard-news

going-soft cash-cropped

outcome:

'This same-day?'

Both:

'As any other day?'

Taking-over: the competing computer-programmes cooperatively collectively *algorithmically* metering *like- a taxicab carrying & insuring business-plan's financially underwritten: & over-insured: under-insured: over-written: or: not-insured at all*:

'An Act of God:'

'Insured? Re-assured?'

WF4.52.

On auto-selling pre-programmed virtual-win: lose: or: draw:

cancelled postponed: & re-negotiated:

*The animal-urge to risk: & win: or: destroy through mistake: err-or: circumstances unfathomable: into living-(0)b.literation nevertheless unconstrained...*imposing: the investment-& merchant-bankers' *(e/n) suring* the values of privatised utilityies' private-equity *stock*-in:

Peoples' currency-bonds bonded-out not-individually personally *self*-owned: by-self: or: other priced-out: cash-back: borrowed on payday *loan* the accountant-Clerks' s*avings*-account pension&life-assurance country-*clear* profit-to: Government-taxes paid-in: or: not: with-held: for-tax(n)ation-state:

Paid-breaks taken-*abroad*:

Suitcases stuffed-full of cash it may as well be except electronically & to-be taken-back with inward investment re-payment in any caughtout: corruption compensation hitting-growth yet hardly covering the or:i:(g)in-all-crime in-cin. sin in-bribes & back-handers': dodgy-deals: millions of them in small-amounts from small-people units for a few: in the billions of fixed-rates false-accounting...

Corporate-Government now cash-in-the-bank cash-strapped stayed out-of-the-bank:

Stayed: Ill-liquidated: stashed-away: unavailable to:

Government or/to: the-People to spend:

Of the-family-business: & as of small-Company-names

factoryies'&Home-Shop(s): *seen* briefly as painted hoarding billboards pasted on the side-of-buildings:

Advertising as along the embankment railway-track: alongside sidings & stations to be passed-through at high-speed: non-stopping:

All else: stopped:

Closed: shrunk: & engulfed by-globular en-largedCorporations' advertising-Banks' currencyies' economic-zone & country-Town passed through:

High-street branches: shop(s) & currencyies'-exchanges: *laundering* as: domestic ironing-out clearing-houses for returns: or: no-return:

'By the end of *the*-day all-will-be-won:'

'Or lost?'

WF4.54.

'Or still stood-still:'

'*This*-Day?'

'Still…'

All investing higher-&-higher with insecure unsecured funds in stocks & insurances: interbank loans: re-insurances: & *re-sales*: within (closed-text) the *listings*: over: & into: almost as suddenly as the whole front-page picture re-pasted into-*memory*:

For the-Clerk far from *assuaging* the culpability of the-other now exposed as the deplorably irresponsible & *reckless* lender:

Not: as-yet wrecked-borrower: *wreaked* havoc-upon:

To the-Banker: the- Clerk cast now as the likely irresponsible yet hapless helplessly indebted: possibly homeless no-deposit poor credit-*rating* history *first*-Time *mortgage*d; &-*possibly employee*:

As in: *Bank-loaned salaried monthly paid-off & to be paidback2back pay-day pay-check paper-money on-screen debt-stocks share-backed: & banked* the-Bankers' newspaper front-page pictorial held-out: taut-& proud as a flag of convenience:

Or as a *crumpled* bank-note:

Opened: to the light as checking the veracity of: F*'oldin'* money:

Bill-fold bank-account the-Clerk knew: & re-turned: momentarily to the hand-held: now re-opening news-*filtering*-screen: newspaper heard again: as the *rustling*-of dry-leaf cadaver:

Outside the carriage: the weather -that inclement: not: *springing* into life or: burning summer yet or: autumnal for the leaves to be freely-falling or: as snow-covered as foraging for-nuts & berries: for the long cold winter:

The newspaper turned crisply inside-out & halved again: Both to the same page *skim*-read by the-Clerk earlier: *pre-registered upfront: next page*:& as world-wide-web free & as-*expected* to be paidfor not-*freely enabled* as-seen with advertisements scanned & scamming papered-over skimmed screen-both *skipped*-to:

<u>The *Insider*-Report</u>:

As of today, there is so much owed, by so many that cannot start to be paid-out or paid-back this day or the next.

This morning the stock-markets across the globe are closed. Once more World-Trade has ground a halt: All credit-debt trading has been suspended until further notice:

The trading of stocks and shares in recent times has left prices at such all-time high-levels that overnight prices have collapsed. Shares and therefore stocks cannot be bought or sold as profits day to day are hit and trading rivals seek liquidation buyouts of each other with severe sanctions and possibly rationing of goods we are yet again in the grip of the greatest global-fiscal&financial-*fiasco* the greatest crisis again ever…again…*again*...

Further down over-the-page:

Markets Closed!

This morning in Geneva there is to be an announcement of the International Conference on Monetary Compliance (ICMC). There is to be a declaration of economic policy & *intent* although no-one knows what this will mean for ordinary citizens. This announcement is expected to stabilise major-global currencies and exchange-rates at some *mutually*-agreed rate to boost confidence in the banking-system Fiscal-Policy and World-Trade. A shared-protocol at Midday world mean-time today by the International Date-Line…

‘There will be winners: & there will be-*losers*…’

looking-up:

The-Banker as from the-Clerks’ *laid-back* attitude drawn from the appended im-*pending… silence…*

The-Banker’s now self-imposed *imaged* point-of-view of the pictured *closed*-markets of the-*Barrel* aka: The-*Cage*:

'*Calculated*-risk? Join the-game?’

'Game? No-*real*-risk then?’

‘Limited-liability only. Only the-*details* to be added…’

WF4.58.

The-Banker: on ear-piece bartered furtively & *openly & loudly & confidently confidentially swapped hand-signals & punched the air slapped-palms & seeking partnered high-fives dropped-down/up*:

‘’We’ are in the six: *seven-eight*-B*illion*...Trillions if you will!' & holding a-hand over the heart openly-palmed & as sat bowed slightly winked a single staring-eye as stooping to conquer with *onscreen* confirmation… *re-directing… con.firming:* password…& printed-off paper-copy as-if: waved-frantically financial-agreement-stipulating:

‘Corporate & Government stock-bonded imports & export…’ as seemingly expertly witnessed as apparently:

‘Only to be signed-off!' lifted-from: the floor brief-cased

revealed laptop lopped looped reeling-off reeking-of as if wreaking-wrecking *havoc* reading-off numbers as The-Clerk now speaking: spoke:

‘Numbering everyone on this Planet!’

'Hell No! No-one-else! No-one else except us!’

The-Clerk continuing:

‘But the markets are closed?’

‘Only the-*detail*s to be added…how many-*Billions*-Trillions more: to-be: made…’

‘Made? Before what? All is Lost?’

‘Devalued: Bought-out: Sold-off: That is the name of the-Game: Selling-off…*cheaply*…’

‘Bought-off: People?’

‘Same: in-di(f)(f).in: ference…’

‘Free-Trade. Have-to: Sell-Goods: To the-<u>Buyer</u>: <u>Seller</u>-Buyers’ *market(s)*…’

‘Seller be-(A)ware?’

‘Deals within deals: Dealt-with: Deals…Done!'

& with a nod: laterally entrusted: undisputed: & further endorsed over-*lengthy* client midday luncheon tied-in *gifting* as charity-in innocence but by guilt-association *expense*-account accounted-for & through now written now *electronic*-signatory *pass*-name & number & two-stage authentication as if but not-actually or: *actuarily*-yet: a matter of public-record:

‘D*etails:* no longer negotiable?’

WF4.60.

‘Or ever-were? Only the-*details* only to be added: The-Market(s) will come thru’…’

The-Banker:

'Then:’

'Then?'

Then:

‘All to-be *ironed*-out today…by the all the-Clerks' of all the-worlds’ works…’ information-*kwiki*: transparent liquid-like sol.(i)cited:

Solid as an assignment: Proposition: Projected: through the air *cloud*-like as before the-bell was rung for-departure…

As a warning to anyone last-boarding the train doors closed: the train-carriage sealed: seated: up-front: aside:

'I don’t know what to make of ‘It’ yet…’ *pause*: *pregnant:*

Then:

'But: I'll *bet* we will find out soon-enough anyway don't you?' from: The-Clerk the-thought snickered *slightingly* to-self: as-if: spoken to self: Then: that *sarcastic* thought: or: was it sardonic? outlined: *out loud*? sounded differently:

As if someone-else had spoken the words instead:

As a gauntlet thrown-down: to be picked-up:

Only as instantly-*realised* now & as at the time-of: *speaking* that short-moment-later as-spoken now *i(e)rritatingly in-tim(e)ating* in-tim(e)idating only-now at the-gamble: n/N… so:-*seemingly… commit*ted-to: the *uncertainty* now at such a communally: yet privately & now seemingly *shared-*ad.venture: seemingly reason-able: or: un-reasonably post-partum as-yet un-priced as-yet only a project(ed.) pro-pos(e)all:-

There would be: a-price & a-cost too:

'Purchase-price & re-sale onward: that's all you need to know:' as-yet an un-bidden offer in-prospect to follow-up the seemingly automatically-accepted challenge: as-yet to be fully realised:

'O.K?'

'O.K:' as well as the-other: each spoken now & heard & now seen:

'No going-back now…'

Both now considering the import of these words: the more thoroughly: *thought*-fully: perhaps than said & heard those outspoken: aloud: as to the-*enterprising* enquiry requiring further-reply?

In-turns? or/not? In-different?

Now the earlier previously *saved* in-memory & as the *first respondent* again: the-Clerk ignoring the *possibility* again of turntaking with another supplementary yet elementary-question:

'Why? Who-is? What?'

'How?'

Puzzlement: seconded now by both-speakers:
Triplicated: as almost-identically mindfully apart reflected against all other on the train:

In the train-carriage: others visible through adjoined compartment &/if not-further apart or: closer-to or: from each-*others' truth*: & in each-others' *minds' mind*: *all this meant what? Exactly? & how soon? How soon: is now?*

How much is-enough? &: *How much is at stake here? Exactly?* as instantly now-both regretting the opening-given to the exclusion of anyone-else in the carriage:

As both-enjoined: as advertently now in a two-way

dialogue: of which at that immediate-point there was purse-persisting yet-only limited-*information(s)*::::…

*

She worked nights: evenings: day shifts: this week it was the late-day shift: or: the Day-Late! as some liked to call-*it*:

From:/To: The Ambulance-station:…at/from: where she drove the-ambulance: as-a: maintenance engineer & assisted at-accidents so-called: First-re/sponder: first-aider but not-yet not-a Super-Medic like some of the other crews had-*had*:

'Be careful: today' he had said to her:

'I-love-you:' & she had replied:

'Same…' joining the a*ccident & emergency crew: trained up in skills & procedures: assessment of injuries: life or: death sometimes:*

Observing vital signs: moving patients safely: onto stretcher or: aided walking: Checking for any changes:

To report-to: The Qualified Clinician taking relevant information: from others carers at the scene:

She: administering first-aid & emergency medical procedures: transporting people to & from hospital: accident & emergency: the elderly & frail to Hospital appointments:

It could be anything: road accident: multiple severe injuries: or: just a scratch:

Taking notes for the medics: & the insurance: & police: if there had been A-Criminal-Act the-Civil Police would be on the scene-of-the-crime: or: the Fire-Service if there had been a fire: or: if someone needed cutting out of a car: Rescuing: from a building roof one two three more storeys up car-park government offices: You name it: Anything: & everything could happen: & did: Never a dull moment: A good job: a great job: She enjoyed & was paid: well: reasonably well: not-poor: Definitely Not-rich!

It could be a pedestrian: or: housebound: head wound: heart attack: to broken toe: In a busy shopping centre: or: on a country lane: Sick baby & worried parent: or: elderly infirm: worried well: or: unconcerned brawler wanting to carry the wound to show-off: not-realising how much blood was being lost!

That is when you needed back-up:

Sometimes a suicide: under a train: not-much you could do for: them: then: bag them up & the under-takers take them away: to the morgue: may later find out the official-cause-of-death by 'crushing' or: 'shattered' in the jargon document dependent:

On the roof: threatening to jump:

'Go on then!' you always feel like saying...

'If you're going to be wasting our time: Ive got children to collect & shopping to do...'

Some others' time...

Some other time...

Once The: 'Bouncy-Castle' *set-up: to: land-in is set-up: on the floor against boundary-wall-to: catch any-fall & the suicide gets frayed-afraid bored & tired & decides to walk the stairs: sorted: esco(u)rted:*

Could be someone fallen down stairs:

Beaten-up in their own home: domestic violence: denying: screaming the odds:or too-(s)cared...

Other:

Unruly: intractable: recalcitrant: not-well-behaved: not-well mannered socio-path or out of control: not-biddable: broken-bones:

not-funny: It would all be reported: had to be:

To the Social-Care Agent:

Housing Representative:

Police: en-forceme(a)nt

They would press charges: if necessary: Must do: ought to:

Some of the things you see…

We pitch-up & patch-up: & tell the story: witness:

Sometimes threatened as well: You had to stand-your-ground:

Emergency blue light: siren wailing:

Steering in & out of that traffic that never seemed to thin out:

or: even give way sometimes:

Still: that was the job:

Worth hanging-onto: planned: going-on to take the Medic.

then:

Para-medic exams: own time; evenings & weekends: &

bring-up: The-children! Check out the vehicle: stocked with

bandages: medical&life-support equipment: ventilator & de-

fibrillator: stored -properly&in-good working order:

Communication equipment to the control-room: where she had started-out: learning how to differentiate one-emergency from-another:

Over mobile radio-telephone: video-link: inside&out the vehicle: & the patients: they would joke heckling themselves:

Checking mileage: speed: safety: on the road: & in situ: clean: New documentation: date: time report charts: name: address if known: distinguishing features:

Check the fuel & oil & water: start up: at the start: : end-of each shift:

Driving licenced of-course: passenger public-service classification: different gross weights & bearing: gear shifts & light: heavy-goods for the larger vehicles: used in public events...Now: though: the regular colleagues' chat: only-*if: there-was: time...was...*

When: NN/NN/NNNN/nnn…

She got in this morning-shift: the morning newspaper: with the Lotto numbers: & television & radio pages: *This make more than a TV drama any day of the week: Fiction & drama* she liked: *a murder: thriller; or: a biography: not-many of them write their own do they?* she thought to herself: *What to write about? I know: Nothing! or: The rest of my life I haven't lived yet!*

The: Accident&Emergency Department Hospital wings were as quiet as usual first thing in the morning: *there's always time for things to change:* 'It always gets busy as soon as I think it's going to be a quiet day!' she called to a colleague: & thought to herself: *turn around & something happens then it all starts happening! You hardly have time to think until the shift is ended: & no overtime-pay!! When did I last finish on the dot: the bell!!?*

WF4.70.

she asked her-self: rhetorically out-loud to the others repeated as every-day: 'When did I last finish on the dot?' answering herself in response with a *thought*ful: but blank thought:

'Never!' they all chanted as if they had done this routine before: *Waiting for the first call: that's when it always happened:*

Some-one driving from home: to work: a van or: lorry driven recklessly: Someone else in a car crash: on the way to work: domestic: accident: or: not:

On: their-way to early-morning deliveries: to a job late for: as if they're the only one(s) on the road: passengers to school: them that has a work-appointment to reach:

With fate: & a social duty ahead Slow Down! You are not-the only one! Think Health&Safety First!

The imperative to keep-working: too-rid(i)culous: too-timely set: time-frames shifts shifting: cannot be late to the game:

So: she could feed self & family; & others could be fed&stay: a-live: their-lives…

Referrals from night doctors; there was always work waiting anyway: no-later than: sooner: the first call of the day:

The drunks: druggies & the otherwise homeless: who often slipped-in: & slept in the waiting rooms during the night shift: had been moved-on: for the day shift to start:

It was not-any different today: although the last call-out had been a disturbance: Some missiles thrown & one person injured: the police were there:

When the ambulance arrived: the crowd had moved away:

The other crew had told them all about it when they got back: The bank had -opened: A queue: a line had formed outside: of staff & customers: with people trying to get wages & savings out: The bank was closed: until further notice: There had been a scuffle between two of the waiting customers over an unpaid unwritten loan & eventually: after others had got embroiled: two or: three lay injured:

Someone: bystander: onlooker: passer-by had called an ambulance:

Several on-lookers came up to them: as they went to see to the injured customer: or: patient-to-be: & the crowd: see-if known to them realising the bank was not-likely to open the-crowd had dispersed to await-any further news & to see if the bank may (some may-say might) open in the afternoon:

She was on second-call but was -needed: The injuries were only slight: but the scene was ominous: an omen it seemed for the day:

If real disaster did-strike she often thought *only enough bandages petrol-electric for a few days: &/only if/that is rationed from the start:*

Only enough food at home: the same: The closer to Big-Shop time: the less there was at home: Go to the local shops: & nothingleft-in-the house apartment really nothing left: at home:

Not: stocked-up recently: & can hardly afford to go more than for a few days at a time without replenishing need:

Everyone was talking about the crash of the stock-markets & the announcement expected at midday:

'We'll have to go to the supermarket tonight!' She had called: after-him: as he had left&*he collecting the children later: after his shift was done; or: the rally: now?*

Suddenly everything seemed more uncertain: & she really did start to wonder: *what this day would bring:* : He met a work-mate at the works: & neighbour walking in the opposite direction home:

'No good going-in…'

the other said:

'They've shut the works again: Remember last time: few

more

out of work: three-day week…'

'The last time: & the time before that!'

'It's happened before!'

WF4.74.

were their blunt replyies to/from each-other: without irony the other replied refencing the **Bread&Cakes** bakery factory they-*both*: worked-at:

"**Bread&Cakes**' closed-down for good this time we reckon: There is a meeting: Midday…' the other continued:

'We'll find out: then!' & laughing:

'See you there!'

shouted: as they passed each other: laughing: at what: they could not-be sure: as-the: children: waving & laughing too&/at: what: they knew not-what: exactly a-waiting midday: *when they may meet-up again*:

'Open for the day:' notice pinned on the school-gate: *thank goodness* had been the immediate *thought* response though-out as *is this fate? Is this the-future?* Although there were *mutterings* & mumblings about whether-the: Teachers&Nursery-Nurses who would actually see their pay& pen(s)ions this month; or: whether any of-*the*: Parents: would be able to keep-on paying for the basic-education public-privately directly or: through public-taxes *never mind the extra-trips& activities' equipment for this & that at least school was open & the children did not-need collecting until he finished his-shift at:*

The Bakery: later in the day: maybe: or: after the: Rally?

'Don't forget after-school!' the Older-One had called after him:

'Half-day today…half-pay!' *their*-Schoolteacher had half-joked: &*laughing*-all to-gether:

'Maybe?! Works are closed today. There's a Rally midday…' wondering what would *really* happen *that*-day.

After sending the text to her about going back home then to the rally later: as the children walked: not-ran: toward the-nursery & the- school doors he out through the parents' gate he went to go to the works then decided to go-back home first: passed by the *other*-shops: nodded & said:

'Hello'

to shopkeepers & customers: standing around inside & outside on the street: up the stairs to the apartment: to their balcony then when he got indoors with the key: shouted:

'Hello?'

'Hello!' responded only just out of habit: & in-doors

switched on the T.V: again: & started to clear the breakfast-thing(s) *away...this/that/(n)either...*

She had already set-off for: work with a sandwich & the last of the bread: she re-calling calling to him earlier or afterwards: then he then thinking: or: *did I say I'd bring some bread home?*

She said: 'I don't care if it's stolen from work! or bought from the shop...'

WF4.77.

She said:

'Don't lose your job over a loaf of bread!' then: he *thought-*

on*:*

Lucky: I got some in yesterday: he thought; or: *sheer skill remembering what she'd told me before I went to work yesterday: & didn't forget! this: same? today...?*

*

As: he settled-down: with a toasted-sandwich: in front of the television: to watch events unfold: he wondered: *or: did I just imagine that? From some other time: yesterday? or: at all: anyway...*

Anyway: what does it matter?

We always need bread anyway then: mindful: *of the mid/day-meeting at work: & later: at the supermarket:* wondering: *what would happen: if there was no work: no money to pay for the shopping?*

WF4.78.

With: worry reserved-for what would occur anyway: which as-yet: he did not-know for sure: for: certain: what would happen this-day: Only what may occur: what could occur; *might*-occur: was all he could really think about:

Home: & a sandwich with whatever is left in the bottom of the bread bin: some jar or: a tub of something: & back to work: or: not-*before the meeting at midday*: reading quickly: scanning the front-page of the newspaper:

Stock-markets in Chaos!

Today, there is so much owed by so many that cannot-even: start to be paid-out, or will ever be paid-back. This morning the stock-markets are closed. Once more World-Trade has ground a halt. All financial currency-credit/debit loans trading-of(*f*) stocks&shares that: in recent times has left prices at all high-time levels overnight have collapsed. We are in the grip of the greatest fiscal and financial-crash cash-crisis ever again and yet- *again*…

WF4.79.

Sitting at home: no hurry: He realised: again: that he didn't *have any-amount of cash with: him: only metal-coin& a couple of paper-plastic notes: that had to be accepted proffered used-up as legal-tender tended tenderly? except now as some vicious aggressive take-overs from faraway Towns&Cities villages nearby*

The cash-card machines would be empty: if the banks were closed: & there had been panic-withdrawing: there would be risk to the security-vans going around & topping them up with new notes now: wouldn't there be: Riots? Money-Riots? Food-Riots?

The money vans will be headed-back or: staying in base: with all the money the armoured security vehicle: bullet-proof cars: dark & light brown: black & silver striped: dusty rumbling over the go slow cobbled pedestrianised street:

Shops either side: walking down the centre he *imagined crowds emerged into the square had emptied the Automatic TellerMachine: well before: so simply locked: & empty:*

WF4.80.

'Under orders no doubt:' accidentally spoken out-loud: thought: *Police escort: & the supermarkets probably would not-be open anyway:*

Since most people paid by credit/debit card: &there was shortage already on the shelves...

They were all virtually 24-hour anyway: virtu(e)-ally food-

feeding every day of the week: month: & year:

It would all be gone: or: *hoarded: or: robbed: Possibly with violence: likely...*

Maybe they will be closed: waiting with-their: stock for...

The prices: to rise? As they had always done before?

*H*e exclaimed to himself: as an image-of: on(e)ly(*e*): *threatened* looting: hundreds: thousands of shoppers checked-out asset-stripping the shelves of everything *paying: or: paying the supermarket could be open for the next day; if everything was sorted-out by then...*

He wondered: *If/&how-much would everything be worth once it was all sorted out? The same as before...but more! What about the food & everything? Corporations' accompanyies' duty-bound to their share-holders first-then: stock-holders: to-put: the prices-up: to their customers to keep their prices down for their customers-as-share-holders' Price-wars! Shopping-Wars! Trade-Wars! Cultur(e)al: diss in-formation... wars mediating customer-consumer with creator-makers selling-on...data:...*

They would have enough to stock-up once &-then be broke again: & if we do not-get paid (enough) into the bank & to-them: then what? &/then:<suddenly he *thought*>less-*calmly(e/e)*:

He had to get some money from the bank: & the mortgage had to be paid: *would the mortgage be paid if the mortgage-company: if the-bank: was closed?*

There was food in the kitchen & he had a little money;

She always had a little-money in-case he spent-his too easily so they/she should be alright for a few days? Day-or-two? Perhaps?

The banks had been shut before: It would get sorted out:

Go: to: the*: super-market tomorrow when the banks would no- doubt be open again:*

After-all:

They are -going to want to lose business is what he said to himself:

'*I get paid so that people like me get to pay the prices to pay-back the shops & factories with profit to pay me again & so it goes around...*' & no-one else there *except*: he & the TV-screen:

On the TV more reports from the stock-markets: around the world: those that had closed: or: opened & then closed: The-City: *the:* Financial-Quarters: just waiting instruction from Big-Business &

Corporate-Government: Market experts: to give their *expert-*

opinion: *minor*-officials from banks & governments made trained traded statements to the effect that banks were closed today: *as if anyone did not-know that by now:*

spec.(u)l(n)ot(e)i®o(n)ation…

Un-less< they were either/or e/v brain-dead; or: living in the

middle of the jungle: or: the desert: up a mountain with no

electricity: no radio-signal: no fuel or: food to cook...

'Government officials are meeting to discuss the crisis:'

The statement at midday would:

'…calm fears of looting…'

never mind looting that had already happened & was about to

kick- off again: somewhere: maybe even here:

News continued to come in from around the world: & was

broadcast simultaneously: Raw & unedited reports on audio &

video from Cities & Country-side cataloguing the unfolding

events: The sound

& pictures visuals graphics of people meeting: being interviewed:

ready to comment on the announcements & their responses:

'Women & children at the railway station: *fleeing*…'

'Temporary…'

shelter tents etc: food & water: in the dust & debris…

&the: like:

'Fleeing shelling gunfire: land-mined fields: cluster-bombed out houses: homes on fire…'

'No Surrender!'

'Out with the-Oligarchs!'

'Down with the-

Governments!'

&:

'Wrong-Rights!'

'Right-Wrongs!'

*

He thought about *Hospital Doctors & Emergency services attacked:*

for trying to save demonstrators: police: or: army casualties misunderstood language: phrases: trying to make more understandable: or: less: catching attackers: or: defenders: it was difficult to tell: difficult to tell what they had been told about those fightingback against Governments: re-(in)sistance: The World-Bank & Global Trade-Markets as necessarily as they made themselves for environmental economic-ecology for freedom&justice all specific&vague:

World Governments & Big Business & Banks' leaders meeting face-face: other-World: leaders via satellite links:

Tele-phones & facsimile machines:

Inter-netted & through screens whirring&humming helicopters buzzed in&out: &landed&took-off:

At the International Conference the most well-known & many totally unknown faces exchanged formalities; beckoning each other forward: back or: sidewards: in gestures of Power-Broking & Politicking:

They were made-to: laugh: coyly in public-at: comments made amongst each-other shook hands slapped backs: Press-conference & delegate meetings: bull-dozed-in:

The Governments & Banks: however: could not-agree; either between themselves: or: each other:

Lines were drawn: & withdrawn:

Re-drawn & drawn-:a-gain...

a-new&still: there were too-many vested in-t(h)e(i)re/interests that divided could not-in one/or: more the next session: get: resolved: satisfactorily to all-parties: Pay&Pensions:

WF4.87.

*Div(id.)ends...beneath The City Road & railway junctions: various junctions to the city centre taped-off: in yellow/**black**: blue/white: red/brown: like a grimy crime scene:*

People coming into The City & towns: & even village centres: Travelling-in: On motorbike & car: Coach: & Lorry: Like a crime scene: they-were made-out to-be:

The Demonstrators: & the-Special Security-Forces:

Outside: & inside CCTV cameras reached the boardrooms; leaking e-mails: toxic enough: high-level Puts & Calls being put-in drop placed: on Present-Index; unmoving defaults: commission interest rates & credit re-probate bait: re-payment: or: not: when to stop-&-start in-game: & out-of: the game: a-gain: Page Up: Page down: side & right & left cursor>>> call: balling joystick socket & lever-aging:

The Real Economy of mills

& factories & shops & fields':

Generating deal-flow: cost-price

benefit: Tax-Revenue: For Social-Securityies' hospitals & schools: roads: & all that: Government branded product-loyalty: different off(i)©/ers: oligarchyies' oligopolies...corporations internal-markets...singlemarkets...continental-to: a few local over-competitively deadly&only a-handful mono-polising mort-g(u)aged to

the hilt:

*

Enough to take technological advance with it: built in obsolescence:

One-Season-Technology: only made to be kept for so long: before the next model between one & two years down the line obsolete constant innovation: healthy: peaceful: price-hikes for relatively for-most: most: the time: maybe all-time:

Royals&Ancients: The Rise & Fall of the Markets...

...everything had to be delivered just-in time used-up sold-up at a frantic pace re-source to rob&rape lands&peoples domi(n)io(N)at(ed.) eliminate the competition monopolise buy-up cartel set the surge-prices high as 'they' like: polarising-still:

WF4.89.

reg.(u)la(i)r(e) reg.(u)(e)lated famili®arity bores: & brings on the-new same-as the-older except-for: in-creasing de-tachment marching-on real-life: politics&re-ligion economics& technology: supposedly protecting civilians& providing: ***Food&Furniture*** *of-life: to make* their *country safe:*

You would think it *would be:*

'To: make OUR country safe!'

But it is not: It is to make their-*country great not-again by making-it:*

'Safe-at-home' or:

'Un-safe': a-broad: overseas seized foreign-nationals…

'And still blood has no-nationality. Countrysides villages towns & Cityies'…'

'Theft! Robberyies' Home-In: Va(i)sion…'

'Make! YOUR country safe-again!'

Country is un-Safe? Bank-Safe? Keep it safe from: fraud-theft

WF4.90.

a-lot of-them&Us: Imperious-dictatorial colonial-cellular:

T*rade War-Games abroad: switching-swapping*

Popular-Peace at home: Peace abroad

Trade War-Games at-Home:

Hierocracyies' hypocrisyies' Theocracyies' breeds contempt:

Con.tempt: hatred:

With pictures & reports: in & from city & town squares here&there:

'The World as One!'

shouted into the air: start(l)ed as news' broadcast: started:

The News Broadcast:

'As WE all seemed to hold (y)Our: Collective-Breath

&a-wait further announcement: Workers arrived to work to join

the meetings & demonstrations that were already gathering in great

numbers at workplaces, towns squares piazza & village street roads

& in: City-Centres…'

As the whole-world it seemed protested Governments at home & abroad in City&Town square: on-line & in front of TV:

The Presidential-CEO (chief executive officer) face appeared; it was difficult to tell if at the beginning or: end of a career-in: almost endless sounding-speech: perhaps on loop:

The-President anywhere anytime looked drawn blood-drained but not-bloodied yet/& al(l)read(y) seemed: *was*-adam/ant no-changes would be made: after the previous offer of *limited*-change had been ig(s)nored: & the speech went on & on: round& round:…

Reports & interviews: speeches: & the chants of gathering crowds: The claims of government officials: politicians & market-experts were supplanted by declarations from people on the ground:

From workplace meetings & city-centre peoples' assemblies worldwide television net-works:

In some places there was the sound of police sirens & others the

rumble of tanks & of truncheons beating on protective shields:

On the TV screen: On the rapidly re-booted Smart-phone add-on screen the picture-*froze*: the phone-book *emptied*:

Error message 303: Invalid connection: Connection: closed:

WF4.93.

WF4.94.

6: Bridge:

As over-crossing an Estuary bridge unnoticed perhaps by anyone-else in the carriage: *Uncared* if-noticed-or-not by anyone *else* at-all: Except now each by the in-*Thrall*: Both Banker&Clerk likewise momentarily inadvertently: & actually advertor(*i*)ally making eyecontact: *flash*-framed each-other: & through the shared-window: as in bright- rainbow & sky-mirror as through each of:-themselves:

The-other: en-*rapt(u)®e(a)*d. recklessly: perhaps: or: this day to be wrecked: as if replicated: refreshing: *relishing* as-then: both focused away both to the outside-world as indifferently: similarly: perhaps: yet *inevitably* differently-from: the estuary-Town one-back towards: other-one: now staring & beyond both towards the as yet unseen: rapidly oncoming-*City:* anyway horizontally&vertically up&down-to: the same outside-world: moved-past: *moving*-past: & through oppositely: & thus as in-evitably differently differentially *viewed* as to what was initially referred to: that too: was soon made obvious:

'Un-charted territory…'

'*Again!*'

'That is what is needed: Fiscal new-product re-packaging staples' cash-everyday needs everyday always new product: get-all

WF4.95.

used-up all needs' to be re-placed sooner or: later: new-fun ideas' functions: new-markets: to-be: ex-ploited…'

*'P*reviously flooded-markets…'

'*Drowned*-out!'

'Drafted-in*to: the-fray:* droughted! Famine…'

'Excess: Moral-obligation sub-rog(*e*)ation Fell! Through-the- roof! On-Fire! Hung from the-Bridge.'

' Experiment! Always! Innovation…'

'Buy-outs. Invent things…new patent-product tweek in-tellectual property internet of things…'

'In-vert things. Re-monopolise market-position…'

'If You can *getaway* with It:'#

'Fiscal-Legal Again: Buy: very-low…'

'Sell-high: Very-High! Asset-strip…'

'Lay-off workers…'

'As customers who can no-longer afford? Sell-off:'

'Sell-Out: The same!'

WF4.96.

'Again!' *crafted* legend on-screen: *names* & places: times:

&/as *instantaneously wrapped*:

'Mental!'

'Meteoric!' *collisioning: folding downwards: & inward fullfelled green-trees brown mud-sliding & earth-quaking shaking bursting volcanic red- flaming: livid*:

'Feel the-Power!'

'So: who wins?'

"'We' do:'

'Not all of us:'

'Ever evens…'

'No: not-all of us: Fair-shares?'

'Not: un-fair ground-investment…

'Needy: then?'

'Greedy?'

'A-Greed? Withold: #'

WF4.97.

‘Fun? Secure investment drive- out buy-up any competition constant battling against fairness transparency&accountability…’

‘Sustainable…’

‘Re-sponsibilityies’…’

‘With Human…’

‘Rights?’

‘Face. Once-lived! Lives again! As an Act of Trust! Fate: To: earn a *decent*-living integrityies’…’

‘In-secure: all-ways…So: who isn't exactly: who is- *normal*? Eh? What is *normal*: eh? You? Company-*Plant*? Eh? Keeping the Company-Line?'

'I was here first? joined before you sat down…’

'But how would I know? Government-officer? That’s ‘It’ isn’t it doing the-Governments’ work: the-Peoples’ work! In the Tax-Office? Government-corridors? Got the ear? Pigs' ear?’

‘Sows’…’

WF4.98.

‘I don’t owe. Social un-Securityies’…’

‘So?’

‘The purse? The purse-strings you?’

'In a barrel of our-own making:’ as *each stock & asset commodity government-bonded share-price passed each sell-by date out-dated:*

‘Mis-*timed*:' as lower & lower price-marker losses across electronic-boards against rows of banked fan-tail desktop screenclosing: *listing:* achronycal & apocryphal foreign & unpronounceable or: home-grown & *familiar*:

On-screen: all falling into the same *raging*-pit: The same *pithy*-core of being: *that*-evening: previously: with prices continuing rising steadily being-bought & re-sold *relentlessly* on-commission &/on: Management-*fee* taken already: contracted:

‘Taken: each time: on-inflated prospect:'

'*Deflating*-prospect now: debt-bailout austerityies’ job-cuts’ social-securityies’ de-valuing societyies c*onfidence*-undone:'

WF4.99.

looking down & into a screen: with *realisation*-rising: dropped in free-*fall:*

‘Unprecedented rises: Then: stagnation now: to: the un-initiated un-mitigated disaster: to: the initiated: just another day's trading: strange: & unknown in-cantation-of: Capitation announced &de-capitation pronounced thereof dis-proportionate blinding *record*-Profit to: profit-warning alerted announced with comparable lamentable-*loss*: *laconic* as compared to a nano-second earlier&no-sooner or: later than:

‘Profits to be re-invested instead?’

‘New Pro-duct logistics chains…’

‘Too-*late*: now: immediate-closure:’

‘There…& then:’

photo-*s(n)apped* sapped: sapper-*zapped*:

Markets closed.

‘No warning?'

WF4.100.

'There-&-then…'

& at *that*-place: as in each *other*-City exchange connected-in: *their:* own-time & place there was for a *change* a stifled stilled: impossible *emptiness*…never-empty ever-*emptiness*…

An assumed & peculiar: & *utter*-quiescence of now religious- *tragic almost*-comical: theatrical proportions: The *Patriarchal-patronising* secular-promise pictured an un-promising candescent screen-saver stilted stilled as on paper-writ:

Markets closed:

crumpled as some witticism *baiting* as some as-yet *unrealised* victim-villain traitorous martyrdom:

'Blown-*up*?'

'Everyday! Knocked-down: Killed-IT!'

'Out of all proportion! What-for?'

'On-track: now:'

toward where dealers in-Global-commodities: wheat&gold: diamonds&cacao: coffee & tea: corn&rice: coal-gas&oil: *fossil*-fuels&rare-metals&minerals' markets: screen-*frozen*:

'Official-Figures?'#

‘All figures are f*alse*: T*rue*? Believed-in: Corruption: Fraudulent: Traceable Buys & Sells…’##

‘Our-own owned-fields’ bought & sold…’

‘What?’

'Yes: how about that? In the-face of advertorial-adversity diversityies’ divestment a Natural-Nature Foundation…’

‘Government keeping Corporation in-line: keeping Government in-line on-line Traders-groups: headed-up:’

‘Lobbying: Lying…laying the ground-for…up-until one-breaks through:’#

‘Corporate confidentiality clause non-disclosure!’

‘Belief! Trust! At the loss of *these* many-people: ‘We’ *few* shall not-*suffer*…’

‘Anymore?’

‘Ever. This-amount: <u>NNN</u>…’ #

‘Or: that: n?' #

'N?' #

'Trust?'

'Or mis-Trust?'

'Deal? Weapons for Humanitarian-Aid & in *dis*-proportionate- proportion: **Rational-Equitable?'**

'What?'

'Rational-Equitable?'

'Falsehoods? Fair?'

'All's fair in-Love&War!'

'Love: *hurts*…'

'So does war…'

'Dark.'

'Web.'

'Of: Be-Lief. More or: Less: Margins: You? Import-Export?'

'Logistics: Goods in-&-out: Stocks&Shares: Supply… &Demand: at the-end: To&from…'

'You got it!'

'No. You got it…' *un-fair shares? &/then never-equitably:*

WF4.103.

never-is anywhere anytime...

'Anyone?'

'Even in *money*-itself: Big-**Bang**! The great-prize is within our

grasp!':

Paused: then:

'We've had: regulation ig(s)nored for some not-all *de*-regulation with an iron-fist&then: with a *velvet*-glove: singing-song of faith: in: *Open*-Markets...'

'*Open*-Society?'

'Means...Free-Trade: '

'Free-Love: If there were such a thing:'

'There is?' *professional proficient-business confidentialsecrets from: competitors:*

'Family:'

'Admissions:'

'Denials: How would we operate otherwise? It is

customary:'

'Who?'

'Customers' confidentialityies'…'

'All-are: Lies…*a re-alignment perhaps*?

'Shareholders' transparencyies'non-*truth* apparently-to: customer(s)'…'

'Standing-still…truth moving none.'

'Or ever then?'

'The-Numbers: *They*...*we*...as: *you*: on-commission: re-evaluation: value for money& management-fee on every sale& buy…'

'Why? Easy…'

'Value-added?'

'To buy&sell regard-less…' *almost*

'If you can sell crap you do: right?'

'Right.'

'Un-sustainable: u-know-that?'

each customer is different:

'Each customer is different…'

'We sell them what they want.'

'You tell them what they want!'

'We all need the goods: the stocks&shares in the first place that other-people want: or/have-to: bury-buyups to stay alive…'

'Are tricked into having to-buy at: N over-cost: n…o-choice monolpolyies'…Money: deals: only: No transaction-costs: only pixels in: time-1-2…3'

then:

'T1-2: Makers&Movers&Shakers. Dis-ruptors of peaceful lives for their own-wealth T3: Transaction-Tax? Not-likely…Zero. How about it?'

'Customer?'

'Allies? Ally? Allay. The-*City* specifically:'

'*SMART?* How do we get there?'

'Where?'

WF4.106.

'The-*City*? Product-Price Placement&Promotion: Penetration: de-velopment: *di-versification*: new-product: costs…'

Outcome?

'Out of the-envelope. <u>Money</u>: The-<u>City</u>: where brokers&jobbers…'

'Jog&break-things: why? so no-one else can have them? Throw their toys out the perambulator?'

'Buyers&Sellers' <u>Buy</u>! & <u>Sell</u>! & make-<u>IT</u>!'

'Make-what?'

'Money. Everyone wants money more of it the better…'

'To: spend on more toys to throw out the perambulator of age? To: better the next Oligarch Billionaire? Why not share?'

gophers' runners-rumoured & listened-in whistles-blown: Bells rung: Trumpets: blew-from: afar: self&other-construed: con.strained (w)rec(k/c)on.(in)structed amorphous-cloud as from behind closed-door newspaper-screened: curtained/off: then: heard-peering out:

'How about a share in the-*recovery*: then?'

'How about *fair* shares then? 50/50?'

'One-to-One: Do not-tell everyone!'

'1-1?'

'Zero-sum? No chance: Time&Money: Work&Play…'

looking-up into the eyes of the original protagonist now turned anta(n)gon(e)(0)(l…)*ist(e)*:

'*Nothing* is for Nothing:'

the-other: the-Banker: looking down into the screen of a half-opened briefcase screen then speaking into a blind yet not-deaf space between them:

'If You don't someone-else wil(e):-l=

action as-if: marshalling-prowess: the-dark-arts horse-back ridden: risen-over<browngrass-roots green-shoots actioning:

'No-*silver*-bullet!' *sword-drawn*...

'Oli-Garch-*Apocalypse*!'

'Soon?'

'Dark-*Mountain project*:' mystifyingly under-mining: transition-culture *collapsanomical*s' comical drilling-down: catastroph-oika *optimism projected…*against pessimism: resurgent emotional reverse shock-doctrinal industrial climate-changing *in-evitability*...

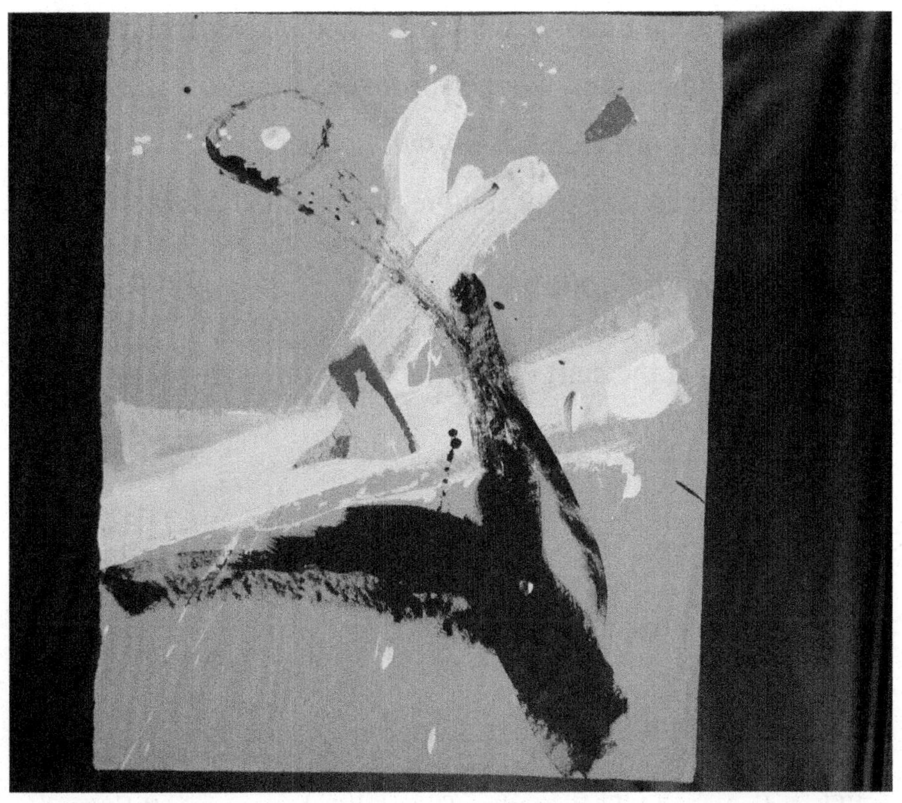

Mu(a)ddled spiritual-cultural debate: of: economic-politick confidence *faith*-boosting happy gamma-rays' *de-coding* brainwaves: into *abstract*-reasoning *memory*:- re-*locating*:

After the event has passed *pasted* into-*history:* acted-out as previously run-*backwards*:on/off/on...before a backdrop of multiple-window screen-*graphics*: a patchy grey-hazing jagged-green shining outward sprouted trail-blazing digital-numerically downward takenrooted routed deeply-inside planetary cent-ring iron&on: carbon-**black** diamanté-*silver*: luminous background: *pixilating*-light screen black & white to-red-*simmering* onto a dark-slate: heat-light dotted: copper-bronze cooling-off *warming*-pastel shades yellow-grey clouds-*softening* over-mountain&hillside as: *the*-City *skyline* re-imagined as print-logo:

The: Rational-Equitable:

ridden-towards as at the start of a *brand* new-day sun-rising:

*

The-Clerk asking now:

'So: How did 'We' get into this mess?'

''We'? What mess?'

'This dis-*array*! This cycle of in-debtedness again? Fast-Action: slow-motion saw IT-coming pile-up! Hit the buffers:'

'Off-the-rails: slow-motion train-wreck:'

'Car-Crash!'

'This *little*-Turbulence…' the-Banker perhaps unexpectedly uncompromising in response to the- Clerks' questioning:

'Wrecking-Ball!'

'There is a market-situation known as Demand&Supply…'

'Where if a company doesn't have enough shares in stock to distribute & sell:'

'Then this increases the price for these as a result: & this is known as a Bull-market…'

'&: this is what we have?'

'Or: perhaps had?'

'Or perhaps a Dragon-market now: *anyway*:'

'A Tiger-market?'

'A growling Jaguar squawking screeching-Macaw Mon(k)eyMarket if you like!'

'A Liger! A Tion!'

'A Lie-ter fire…Bonfire of the Vanities! 'It' doesn't matter what you call 'It': The bigger picture: *thinking* outside the-box:'

'The-Cage?'

Outside the carriage: momentarily looked blankly: thought & spoke: the-Banker:

'If you like: The *reverse*-situation:'

'What? Supply*:* then: Demand?'

'Inter-linked supply-chains…' *chained...*

Not getting the reverse-irony from the pen-ultimately *closing*-under a bridge: *continuing* out the other end of a subway:

'Logistics' light! Wake-Up?'

'A _*Bear*_-market?'

' This is when there is an increase in quick-sellers…'

'I know *that-t*oo: *cheap-cheep virtually*-virtuously?'

'& a-fall> in-buyers' affordabilityies' to-trade: stocks'& shares'…go-to…'

'The-money mostly…'

'Only the-money? Food-Cash? Whose? Yours?'

'Mine?'

Bluntly:

'Every-bodyies' itemised-*lists*:…'

savings: pensions: investment: salaries& wages: day-rates' ...

'Gig-Economy without protections…'

'Who needs those? This is now what we now have:'

'Risk?'

'Shared?'

'Share? The International-Banks: & Economic-Zones: Government& Corporations'…'

"It' is a Global-Market!'

'Now the bottom has fallen-out of it…in a closed-market the only way to win is to take from the bottom…'

'En(d)trop(h)yies' stealing from the poor to make the rich…'

'Richer?'

'Every…day…'

'To: day…'

*

The-Train moved slowly out from a glass & steel raised slab of the new edge-of-Town: main-line high-speed railway-platform running alongside the banking blank back of high-street shops: & the station car-park: awaiting return:

Into harvested-fields & open-grazed pastures below remaining precipitous pine-forest alongside planted-poplar windbreak: shielded through the trees: the new days' sun appeared: speared; *blinking* awake burst! through the carriage breaking-beyond the blue-grey staged: & staggered: rolled & ranged:

From the east-*peaked* settling yellow-orange onto the westernhills: Shadow-flanking purple-green valleys: & up-country the farmed grid-framed plains where the day was already begun:

Grey-whites as if steam-lifted across a drying-up estuary in *thin-rain* spluttering over an elevated iron-riveted painted girderbridge: Built-on: pillars of a deep-red local stone & brickwork: arched&*breached*:

With the Suns'-rays the train rattled-on:

Emergent: as through a fog: over a beached river: onto the other-side: of a ravenous: gaping-gorge: Over-spilling through the outskirts of a recently built-up ancient sea-harbour & river port:

Sub-Urban: edge-of-Town:

High-rise housing-project: industrial-units: chimney-stacked…

Business-park: & shopping-mall: Home-furniture: & motor-car showrooms: Salesrooms: cheap-hotel & motel: Link razor-wire fenced: chained-in: a horse-paddock: gated & pad.locked:

WF4.115.

Ad.jacent to a blue-green to red-waiting train-crossing signal: a freight-train: privileged-over passenger: passaged prerogative: *thundering*-by *that* morning conjoined passenger-train: trundling along for: now:

Beside a chequered black & yellow train-crossing arterial hottar-road weighted-heavy & ever busy-with: Omnibus & coach: cycle & motorcycle: car & caravan-trailer & engine articulatedJuggernaut: Container-shipment on-board: onto & beneath the overpassing concrete-highway into: & out-of-Town:

All: traffic travelling with one accord: To-&-from galvanized corrugated iron steel & zinc-tin rooves roving between brick &cinderblock doorways loading & un-loading bays:

Beneath canopy entrance-coded & secured air-extracting: for the most part: to the outside world unseen windowless between belching cooling-tower: pylon-linking electric-welding workshop:

Engineering: factory-crafted: machined & h&-made goods: **Food&Furniture**: packaged warehoused & shipped *virtually* to-&from the-Cityports&portals: co-modifying in-return stock-yards stacked-up in-exchange value-assured & awaiting transport to-&from: **Home&Over-seas**-seized:

From the-Banker: a printed-card handed-over with writing seen:

The: Rational Equitable:

Economic: Effective: Efficient:

Nothing else except for a City skyline logo spelling-out:

TheRationalEquitable:

'R/E's? You think this is *Easy* too?'

as practiced before:

The-Clerk given-taking & reading the-*card*: noting:

'Import&Export Currencyies'...'

'Scarcity...'

'Ill-Liquidated...'

'**Boom! Boom!** & **Bang**! Again! **Bang**!! & ***Bust*!** No-debts: as such: you see? Owing-Others...You?'

'Of course owed. They would not-be debts otherwise...'

'Bought-up: See? Cheaply...' *Falling*-in grad(u)ally:

'Bail-Out: Sovereign-Debt bought-up ailing currencyies' ...'

'**Business&Governments** owed military-owned civil-servants' serf-dom. slave-pay Owned: Bargain-basement: Credit/Debt- driven...*again*...' given re-mit *rent-leant* learnt: *Free*-running now on all cylinders The-Banker let loose: re-covering: on the tracks: next-steps:

'To: spend-on: the Stock-Market Prices shared-out always at some point in the past...' *minimal seconded in seconds triplicated:*

'Like *the*-last night?'

'Remains'-high:'#

'Others' collapsed completely:' ~#

'Buy them up! You got IT!'

'No: you got it. All I have got is debt...' as the previous evening passed into-night & into *this* day:

'From First-impact! trading instantly: as a body collapsed:

In: the-moment *between* open & closed: *fortune*s made *retained*:& fortunes lost:

In that brief second-take before the closure: the final roll of coins landing face-down or: tail-up…across the-Globe:

Without the *liquid* monetary-assets in the banks to pay: or: repay: to cash-in: for-the:

*Asset*s to be bought-off:*whole-Corporations* brought-down: Government(s) too: true:'

'Even?'

'Private-Equityies' to-be: sold-on?'

'What-for? Services rendered? Money? Assets bought? Interest?'

'Profit? Depend-on: Governments'…'

'Lending-rates with-what? With non-*existent* credit? On-paper…'

On-screen:

'Government-Debt…Public-Private: Equityies' Assets! Instant-winnings! Bountyies' from: God!'

'All Puts' made-*must…'*

'Stay-on! Stalled!'

'Precisely!

'Business as Usual? Fixed!'

'Only! *Nothing*: is moving…'

as if behind a dropped paper-curtain raised *hidden*-heard *annoyedanger*: dopple-gang de-ranger:

'Since the inevitable: Pay-up-& Get-out!' the-

Clerk now sub-claused:

The-Banker:

'Currency currently & con-currently worthless in name in shares' worth only the original-cost value of the product…plus: transaction-fees pure-profit for nothing except the introduction feasibilityies'…'

'Goods…Stocks&Shares: Money…'

'**Food&Furniture**…' *associated*:

'Relative to others!' not-of-themselves *toxic*-stocks but

toxic-of: whatever *noxious*-currency they are being bought&sold-

for…' *toxic-carbon token-economyies' heating...choking not-breathing*…breath(*e*)d-in foul-air:

'Oiling the engine…'

'Rocket-fuel!'

'Oxygen of life: Hydrogen in the water metallic-catalytic converter electro-lytic…'

'Exactly!'

'Or:-*not*: as the case may be:…'

'Utilityies'…! n/(*e*)got(i)able shall we say?'

'The-Goods?'

'Stocks&Shares.'

'The-property of whoever has bought or: sold them then?'

'As: monied-shares or: stocked-them in the first-place locked-up…'

'Government-Bonded Guaranteed…'

'Import-Export: got to get-to: *them*.'

'That is others' work-a-day.'

‘Got to get them moving…’

‘&/*the*-only way-to do-that?’

‘What?’

‘To-do *that*-is:?’

‘My-Way.’

*

Looking-out of the window: Across oil-field pipeline: gravel pitted hillsides: concrete cement-based conveyer-belt-brick-buildings smoke-stacked flues’ venting:

'With wider & wider differential-*ratings*:'

Deliberately looking again: forward through the window: directing the gaze:

'Making-money stalled un-sold: as-yet:’

‘Bought. n-bought: The risk-of…’
‘Lost between one day & the-next:'
'Bonded between one-place&another:’

‘Sell-by date gone-off:’

Looking out the window:

'Until this day when the-*Bear roared?'*

'Or clawed Its way back…'

'The markets?'

'Goosing! Taken to the air or whatever…'

'Crash landed!' & any other animal-analogy thought-of

statuesque yet mis-represented: the other-wise rapidly turning…numbers turned-off & unrevealing drowned-out surfaced exploded in slow-motion in-pieces:

'Get: shot-down!'

market-marker board: & screen-seen pictured: mobile-camera photographed: on the train-travelling from where the other world stock-markets' early-day trading had or: would have already begun: with the hammering of ancient cast-metal: a brazen-gong *heard*:

A knotted-tied rope-pulled a whistle or: an air-horn or: an electronic *buzzer* air-vibration-*release*d…warning-signal…

Red light:

Black: as the night: yellow-red: to blue-green: as to the light of day: As when the field or: factory-hooter blasted pale pastel-*yellow* rising over the horizon: As at the-beginning: & then again the closing-of-business trading: the-previous-day where-ever 'it' was: trading-constantly throughout the world: around the globe: & then as with each evening: following-on: to the final-days' trade: & the next un-started:

'*Final*-Trade?'
'What?'

'Was it correct? or: not? Accounts? Profit?'

The-Clerk checking-accounts' screen: clicking:

<Accounts?:*closing*:*instantly* closed-down: Then:

>Credit? *Advanced?* Profit or: Loss in…T1:T2…

The-Banker:

'T3. Aces-in-their-Places! Done-deal: Commission! Profit-margins? Bonus! Stays: stay-put:'

'Until they are Put:'

'Again?'

'All that is in the-*Future*…'

'Exactly:'

'Now:'

‘So; it doesn’t *matter*: now? Ker-ching! Blinging!' behind the scenes: stabilising: then immediately back onto *the:* Dealing-room floor:

'Leveraging core-competencies:'

'Play: for-today?'

'Pay-for: today.’

*

The-Train-trolley-bought brought coffee & tea snacks delivered paid -by un-authorised carded-machine paid-for with *cash-only* to: the table between:

'Well: Here’s the Deal:’ *un-questioning intention anymore:*

'Further-loans at fixed-*assured* rates:’

‘Assured?’

‘To re-finance the debt?'

'Cover possible-*loss*es: surely compensation-cover

guaranteed?’

'Never: Never use that word!'

'What compensation?'

'Life? Guaranteed?'

'Insurance?'

'Surety of Inter-bank inter- governmental…'

'*Rate*-fixing…The International Conference: fix(ed:)-interest

& exchange rates will take care of that: A declaration expected

today…'

'Midday?'

'Or thereabouts:'

Re-called: Stepped-up:& in: again:

'Yes: I know that!'

'To stabilise major Global-Currencyies':'

'Exchange-rates? I know *that*-too: At some lower>*fiscal*-

rate a-*greed*…'

'Or not?'

'Higher?'

'& lower…'

'Now! You got it!'

'No: you got It.'

'At the same time if *You got it they got you…*'

'They got you?'

'They?'

'Who? What if *They* cannot agree?'

the-Banker looking-up sharply & out of the window as if there were nothing there:

Where farms & factory-buildings: homes: & retail-parks: *flash*ed-by:

Held:

The-Clerk: as if sub-claused:- caused again: now:?

As if rightly left out-in the-cold:

The- Sun: *warming* hillside outside: shouldered out of the window reflection: moving-on:

Attempting: open-jawed to fill the *void*: but no words came out: *dry*-mouthed: & with an intangible uncertainty fuelling feelings unfamiliar-*anxietyies'* both: yet: not-so obviously one to the other again anyway re-torting to the-Bankers' in-complete: statement: & asking again:

'And if *They* cannot agree?'

Paused: On*e)ly(*e*)…

'A-Greed?'

'A-Greed.'

*

Not-even: *thought*-(a)bout:

'Of-course! Which they must Do!'

'They will?'

'*Their*-will of course they must!'

'Otherwise?'

'We: Will prevail!' photo-shopped elastic-banded *sprung-back* missiles blasted into hordes & hoards of hired mourners massedcrowds: gazing at a poster ad.vert: both:

'Stock-market…'

'Super-market…'

'Hyper-Global marker-markets at: points & places:'

'Gone!'

'Everyday shopping? Going to the cinema: theatre:'

'Bear-drowned: makes the-odds?'

'Bull-fight?'

'In money?'#

'Some may-not return…'

'Fish out of water:'

'In the soup:'

'In the swim. Some adapt:'

'Adopt. Some do not:'

'There is the fight:'

'& then it is over: the-fence.'

WF4.130.

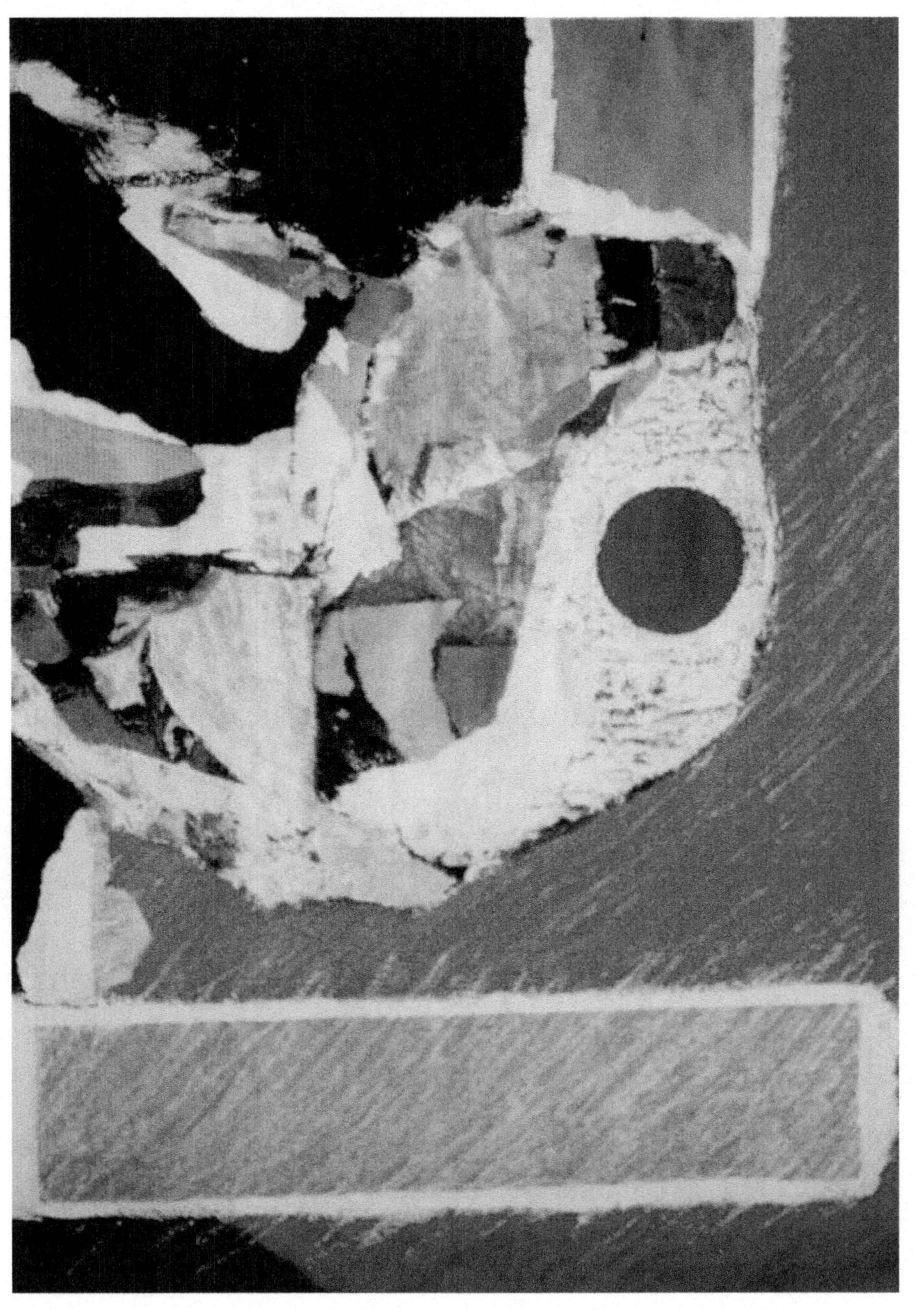

'Then: there is the *mental*-fight:'

WF4.131.

'Well-Being? Real or: (i)magi(n)(ed.)?'

'Over: & over: in-*detail*?'

'A lie?'

'Changing the-story:'

'*Bear*-witness…'

'Ohhh Bullish! Only the-*Truth*!'

'Truth will prevail…'

'Whose? There is no-truth only constantly moving-moments…no-Absolutes: No-Gods to rescue us or: Justice to rescue us only ourselves will-*prevail*:'

- No-Goods?'

'No-matter how *unlike*ly:' driven: as being still: waiting for things to happen:

Re-action: Response: Consequences: Action: Un-prepared: Pre-pared: Pre-dictable: Un-predictable:

'Price-war?'

'Trade-war?'

'Under-wraps. Averting Trade-Wars is what the conference is about: but for us everlasting everyday:'

'War? In your favour?'

'Sure:'

'Only?'

'If right & wrong cannot settle the argument:'

'It won't:'

'Then profits will: All things to all:'

'Profit? From loss?'

'Last-Years' Patent-<u>Profit</u>: available worldwide: from shared academy-styled: *research*: Big:-Business:*shares*-fallen:' as un-known from: known before: a-*moment*: then:

'For later-life: health: & retirement from work: for leisure:'

'Compensation for life-insurance pension…'

'Investments kept for-eternity?'

'For-Family?'

'Could be:'

'Family-farm&/or:…'

WF4.134.

'Apocalypse-War? Something?'

'As a *small*-Business *flourishing*:' *mocking-other?*

Seriously:

'Public-Payback time!@The Big-banks? National & Private: Inter-National Global Companies: The-People in-Corporated:'

in the *background*:

'In the background?'

'Species' Naturally-(s)elective...'

'Fittest-Bought: Natural *de*-selection...sold...'

'Circular...'

'Sanctions!'

'For-what? *sanctimonious goose-food gendering-(g)anderrr...back*ground: *pulling* the strings...issuing-*suggestions*: fore-ground modelling make-believe modest *debt*-reminders:cash-flow cut-off threats *if*-necessary...bargain-Trade-*agreement*s::::...

'Owners' Share-holders' d(i)v(i)d-end (i)-custom errrs

last…'

'Trade-ins?'

'For what?'

'Swaps:'

'Flipped. For: <u>Fuel</u>-flow cut-off: subsidy: tax: call It what you will: 'It' gets more-*serious*:'

'Medical-supplies?'

'Food: Trade-*stop*page. Food-shortages: & water: how about that?! Medical-supplies!'

'One-Way Sanctions?'

'For what? Food?'

'Stable *healthy*-economyies'…'

'Whose *Social-Stability?'*

'Or war? For: *fair*-Financial-agreements…'

'Peace-Treatyies treating…crisis-Capitalist Central-Command Economyies' Communist state(s): even merely *slightly*-Social inclined for the good of others or only-self?'

‘To: stay-in: The-Game. The **World Bank Group (WBG)**:’

‘United-Nations?’

on the sly-*real* sky-line glanced: surreptitiously or: *openly* simply un-challenged:

‘That is down to others’…’

‘Politicians’ People-Buy.’

‘Only if they’re already shown to be winning…’ looking-down into a lap-*emptying*...’

‘Or Sell? Buyers’ or: Sellers’ Market?’

‘Weaponizing: Protecting personal interests…’

‘Defending interests…’

‘Sell! Sale-on! **Boom! BOOM!!**::’

'…& **Bust**:’

'& **BOOM!!** Again!'

'Until it's time to go **Bust!** again:'It’ is all about when

you get-in & when you get-out:’

‘An end to **Boom&Bust?**’

The-Banker: accordingly affordably: breaking-out of the cyclical-contortion if for nothing-else in-particular: except attempting-*testily*…a/n: expla(i)nation of:

'The customary re-normalising-*writ* to be *re*-presented: Of what may be implied: in-Realityies' *terms (NNN/nnn/...)*:

'Un-realistic?'

'Interest in Monetary-terms:& that which will decide the-Day:the: Periodic-*Existential*-crisis of Investment banking':'

'Daily 'It' seems:'

''It' is only having that Competitive-edge::'

'Advantage: Naturally: Natur(*e*)ally? I see it in you:

You're a Natural!' *a bit too-sarcastically: or: was it cynical: sardonic or even irony meant literally*:

'Fixed-on lower to higher *interest*-rates: Keep interest-rates higher-to…'#

'Too-low?'

'To-be: honest.'

'& otherwise? You mean you haven't been up'til now?'

‘Too honest: perhaps…’

'Who? All of us?’

'Or none:’

‘Everything I say is false:’

‘You *think*?’

‘Interested?’

‘Commercial-confidentiality:’

‘Never mind…’

‘Only if True?’

‘Eh? False? Only natural! Lyin’ & cheatin’…’

‘Human nature:*Animal*-spirits…’

self-recognised: self-fulfilling in the glow of a *naturalistic*-fallaciously held-privately:& publicly- renewed self-*admiration*:

'’We’ prepare for 'It:’

Me(e(a)ting) head-on:

‘Scheduled-in…’

'On what?

WF4.139.

Human-conditions as commodities? *E*- motional…

'*This* Stock-Market?'

'Debacle'

'Based on the facts…'

'Do you? or: could you have been?'

'As in preparations? for a drought-flood-draught-wind…'

'Fingers-wet burnt…'

'Free-fire failed…'

harvest?

Hard-Software crash? That's it isn't it?! Cover-up? Conspiracy? Woke-up! You want <u>Me</u> to fix the software?Fix the algorithmic numbers-to-names...

Cyber-ne(tic hard-hat compromised going-down faster & faster as threat caught-up with no-one notices:until the final second: at the last minute...

'Pledge-Price. Governments *print*-more from

millions2billions to into the 3-trillions in:-Over-flated…'

'Planet-People for-Profit only IT-is*sss* at the-margins:'

snaking...snake-oil...

'Asset-Commodities Goods not-only but mostly carried-by sea across oceans showing up on screens' satellite image(s)' tracked&traded::::traced:::: (N/nnn…'

'Trading-Ships Merchant-Vessels Royal-Exchange…'

'Sovereign-Currencyies' colonise former-colonies' Colonising-Independence: Capital-con:trolling… Imperious-Presidents' *people* as-thing(s):-= In-Transit: Halted: Portside…'

'High-Seas protected armed overflown G(lobal)Posit.ion(i)(n)(g)System/at(t)ic-ally knocked- out…'

'Co-ordinates shorting:long-term credit/debts…'

'Seconds sometimes:milli-seconds: moving-on: day-rated interest-rates on commodity-asset man(u)facturing pro-duction sales'loans marginal…'

squeezed…Power-up buttons pressed:

‘Day-tops long enough to make a packet & move-on: selling-on: sooner/later matters not to private equityies’ land-holdings product rates of exchange of course: this will be-*done* by midday…what is that game you have there? Warfare4: Call of Duty?’

‘Trading-Game…’

‘Trade-War Game?’

‘Trade: Game the same:’

‘Costs…Weapons? Ammunitions…’

‘Bullets & Bandages…Bread: Lives…’

‘Jobs & mortgages insurance itself un-insured…’

‘What against-War?’

‘Against-Terror making terror: Reign-of-Terror going-*down*:’

‘Stock share-prices?’

‘Saving-Game…’

'What savings?'

'Familyies' business:*livelihoods*:work-loans:&-Home? The Credit-Debit Store *loyalty*-card? Mortgaged? & the pay-day loans & debts that go with?'

'So: what are the we supposed to save-for? To be starved into submission like subservient pariahs? To be homeless?'

'So: mortgaged: then: no-rent Credit/Debit card? or: nice-slice-cars own anything else?'

'Shop-cards? Loyalty-cards?'

'Down-to: *trust:* again: *they* don't want you to own them they only want you to *owe*-them numbers…'

'What *the*-Shops or the-shops?'

'Banks? Investment-Houses? Pensions?'

'Insurances? Do We not-*own* them?'

'For: Life? *Could*-do. *With shares: pensions: & insurances? Of course:…*The-Banks: do not-want you to own them they want you to owe them check lending-rates low-now they need something-else to profit-from…'

'Government Bail-out that is *all* they want:'

'So then: You have to pay-off as little as possible but/t: regularly under *de*-regulation to: regulate-markets…'

'A-gain?'

when the clouds clear:

'Flat-screen Smart-TV? What about *that* gadget? Bought: or: borrowed? Vehicle? Any other Property? Loans? Shares: & stocks? Insurance? Stock-up each week? less?'

'What-do *You*? Want-to: *know-that*: for?'

'<u>Credit</u>-card? <u>Advance</u>? What You owe? Already? Plus…'

'What?'

To: any cross-trading traffic immediately curtailed blue-green *cross- trades* as another parallel & crossing-tracks passed & rattled& rolled-over like passenger & freight-lines passing like ships in the night like aircraft in the-*perhaps* moonlit-dark starlit-passing that (NN/nn/../) pre-vious: night: NN/nn/../)

'Margins-called:' *tipping-point:*

‘*Past-Profits*:' past:

silenced: skulked: sunk: & lights turned-out:

Screen left-on: referenced:

'*Markets-closed?*'

The-Clerk: to the-Banker:

'Close of play?’

'Time to Pay:'

The-Clerk:

‘Time to Play?'

*

The-Clerk moving around tapping toes & hands mumbling: to: *self or: to the screen-talking unawares into the earpiece microphone replacedlead talking to someone?*
Talking to…
Who? Listening to what? Is that: singing-along? To what song?

‘Watching *the*-Game?’

‘What-*game?’*

7: Titanic!

Watched-in: window-manifestation: man(u)fact(u)r(e): info®m(n)at(i)on: on-line Global-*News* updated: the-Banker puzzled as/at the-Clerk head-down: no-further eyeballing body-contact & the-Banker *shuddered* at the *thought* of the-Clerk maybe getting ahead of the so(u)m€ any-<u>*Game*</u>:

'LoL'

'Ha-ha: There: You have got it!'

'No: you have got it!'

'No! You have got 'It!'

WF4.146.

‘What? The ball? the-outfield?’

‘The umpires whistle?'

‘Managing the game?’

‘Calling time?’

‘Referee!!! Time-out! Foul! Yard…Metre-line! Out-the-Park!' dropping-down: the eyes: leaned slightly forward: looking into keenly:

<Enquire-upon…@:from the *Market-place*…

>Pricing…guidance…mortgage/rent…pay…skills C:V…:fixed…fixing:overheads…Capital-amount: Your-Balance-sheet:…

>>Credit:plus/*minus*:Debit:*indebted*:to::Bank of You::*closing*:

‘Crashed:Again!’

‘Fouled-up: There is -enough Value in the-*Economy*:’

‘The-Economy? Whos(*e*) To: pay: Capital-*assets*: list:to selloff…then to cover the Owed: owned-amounts: to: *lists*:outgoings:that must be-*paid*:’

'Including *hoax*-loans & *overdraft*-agreed…'

'Account-closed? Need-*cash*?'

'I know:'

'Owed? By Who? When? Why? Because the-debt you *start*with is the-one you are stuck-with: Already: worth more: or: less than one-second ago…not only increasing the-*debt*…but decreasing the chances:of-*recovery*:as *the-likelihood...*probabilityies' of that*debt* ever being paid-off: Made-off…over-seas seized sourcingforcing your Currency to be de-valued:'

'Which means?'

'Im-Moral jeopardyies' hazard un-accountable excessive-risk…uder-valued: You get less-for-more: For-example: when you spend your currency overseas on-*imports* to *your*-country y(our): *exports* are priced-higher to others as to yourself named: *list:…*'

'Im-ports that you need: are expensive: to you…'

'Only what I need…'

'Nevermind the-*Luxuries*? Even-<u>*you:*</u> need luxuries fast-car…import-ex/port?'

'Export-im/port?'

<Your-Imports::Nn:pay-off:that You need to payoff:

>Your Loans: exported-list:& your:

<Bank: over-draft:N/nnn:& buying the things you need from abroad…are expensive…Nn:

>Buy currencies?'

'Exporting:…' portable:non-

fungible…

'S©(i)en©t(i)me(a)n(s)(t-T)al…making:…'

'Money:'

'What money?'

'A lot: The Brick-*value…'* changed:

'Anything:cars:TV-station:your home:loaning money to buy with: Insurances' pensions' those Corps shared in the billions by your bank & building society:'

'Corrupt?'

'Fraudulent…'

'Fair?'

'Rational(*e*)?'

'Equitable? For-All that?'

'Nah…most: Shopping-home taken-out short-term credit-loans then to pay-off other loans:'

'Casino…crashed?'

'Never: Break the bank *then*:'

'Break the trust:'

'Mugged then:'

'Slugged:'

'That's about-it buying others' currencies…'

'Selling?: Yes/N0? Cash-account:*in the-bank*:'

'Un-cashed:' *then un-cashable until the numbers stay…the same:*

'Cashed-out? I don't know! Why would I do that unless I was going on-holiday! On Holiday! @:? Exports/Imports: n/N not-N/n:travellers-checks…'

'Government Bonds bail-out d*e-values*: Development-funds Global-Bank Inter-National Monetary Fund(s)' United-States' Re-Construction&De-Velopment@leveraged loans' assistance ending extreme poverty shared prosperity globally financing multi-lateral investment guarantee dispute settlement…'

'Yours?'

'Every-ones'…'

'Others' against yours' … '

'Own-owned:'

'Familiyies'?'

<N/nnn:print-more-currencyies' Government-bonds?'

>*Quantitively*-easing…

'Printing money:Sovereign Interest-rate rises food-inflationary! Cost of Living crisis…' peaked slowed-down…

'*De-valuing value of life…*'

‘*Necrocracy*-Same! Privately owned government public bonds/debts un-limited life writing-off *other*-lives…’

>Debts: Nn: *de-fault…*

< *Sell-off? Y/N Y. Now? NOW!*

‘With Dignity!’

‘Defeat! with valour!’

‘Devalues yours against them…in monetary-terms…’

‘So: the monetary-value of the currency against?’

‘Others’ currency…currencyies’-zone?’

‘Yes: or: National-Banks’ Country-Zones::*list(s)*…’

‘Profit-Interest Financed-debt (PIF’d) the only-way?’

‘For: the-money de-functionalityies’ now fungibilities’…’

‘Rent-borrowing…’ on assets accumulators’ co-lateral:

use: re-turn-ow(n)ed. not-owned permanentlyies’ over-time:

paid-freely eventualityies’ share-owned in-gradation to:

zero-sum expense-expanse owned:

for-ever…

WF4.152.

< Credit-accounting debit-entry value:<>in-crease debt>>> journey-journalised: trip-tricking lending-out propertyies' owned asset-based cost-plus co-lateral deferred payments'asset-financing stocks&shares the-more rightfully-owned the-more… responsibilityies' to: societyies' absolute god-given or: adaptive reasonable natural-laws accumulating-wealth health pleasing-to: consume give-away to: charityies' stealth:

> Credit/Debit historyies' to: eternityies' meeting financial-needs with integrityies' trust-worthy honestyies' equi-vocalities' certainty-of-purpose sharing-in profit&loss not to invest-in: weapons-of-warfare gambling-lives credit-historyies' deposited terms of agreement(s): factor(ed.)-in: asset-ownership stock-holding shared profit-revenue gained from activityies' such-as: real cost-of transferring funds expenses incurred such-as: food&drink: needed to sustain- life/lives: taxes&inheritance on: death(s): owner of asset investment or enterprise: non-fungibles' unique selling-points inter-change abilityies' onland: silver/gold

cash-worded@ symbol-symbolising: Goods&Stocks of:

Food&Drink/Bread&Cakes tool-making trinkets charms

ornament costume ad.d(uress/sub-tract (ed.)) value: fungible

inter-change abilityies' re-placeable numeric-allyies' materiel-

Home: paper-wood/money metal-coin/money of such a nature that

any one-part may be easily re-placed by another equal part amount

or quantity (regard-less of: *quality*) co-lateral da-mage…

calculation on: breach-of-contract: insured pay-out pay-back

credit/debit account for natural re-sources:

stone/brick/wood/metal/

(s)oil/wheat/rice nice people-money capable of: mutual-

sub.stitution

situation(s) war-times inter-changeably destroying destroyed-for:

any-future prooving proof-us as-of: (NN/nn-nn/nn/nnnn):

The-Clerk: clicked: looking-down: in-to: *anguish*: or: *fear*: or:

anger@deprec(i)ation but-with: de-preciation:

‘Money is good…’

‘Never have enough…all the-money in the world!’

‘As it is…’

‘All the-money bet-on: all the-world(s’…’

Forensics’ *the*-real: Crime@Scene Investigation(s):

<Imports-Exports::for currency & the stuff currency buys:this is more-important than the actual goods' value of the goods:

‘*The*-currency?’ *list*:

‘Gas-oil pipeline…’

‘National Infra-structure…’ canal-bridge seized to the open-sea built over muddy marshwater concrete-passage flooded-access limited-global long-way around:

> What do you want to trade-for-currency?

< Commidityies’ want(ed.) to: trade-for: stand a-lone currencyies’ trade-hall market-stand:

> De-fenestration-currencyies: : basket-case…

transparencyies' open-doors slammed-shut:

<Out-the-window!

>De-forestation currencyies…

<The-Oceanic Global-Trade…

>Reducing: N/n:river-bridge canal-to:…*block: list...*

<Plastics-Pharming…Farming…GoTo: The-Bank's: *list*:: For: *The-currency Money...*

>To pay-off the Sovereign-credit/debt…

<Loan-credit: *On-paper?*

On-screen::

'**Rational-Equitable**:' the real-world: on-screen:

< Shares:*getting-there*:-of the National-Wealth:

>S*uper-subs*: US/Australia/Canadian Dollar/Yuan-*Mindi Yen*/Sterling*silver...*

<Gold-R&/new-Ruble/new-Dinar/ convertible-Peso/ Rea & Rupee: Shekel/R(i)yal…Euro:

for-bearance to the holder bearing of your:

‘Z: Zombie? Me?’

<Servicing-debt…choking-off further lending: be-heading *clean-cut ripping out the guts in front of boggling-eyes as they used to do:* *bart(e)(a)ring* internal-currency straight-swaps for-profit: between financial-institutions&zones to settle a contract(ed.)

(*i*)deal…

>OK: *Rates*-available: *list*…as above: or: below: other-short: (ed.) to long-term deposit: (ed.) may be made…to: be-used-up:

<Savings::Credit:in the-Bank to be: : made: use-full: *as we and only we make our-selves others' make them-selves…*

>Lending-for *investment* at a *reasonable*-return or: simply fore-going fight/fright freighting foreign-feigning: *fore-closing*: The cash-till action:

‘Going-down!’

'Sinking-ship:'

'Titanic!'

The-Banker held onto the newspaper: brief-cased opened screen: Sat back: where had been leaning-forward: in some kind of *reverie*: Looked-over: & stared the-Clerk directly in the eyes: & between & around the other less-experienced in the ways of the world: Shiny-suited silver-grey not-dull-*charcoal*:

The Banker: a sharp-suited charcoal-grey power-dresser rotund in-parts: like a tailors' dummy sharp-suited: three-dimensional 4G strung-out: as a hand-glove puppet: to the Invisible Puppeteer:

Staged-stood sound-designed: as-seen self-motivated moving…synchronous photographic-form: breathed-in:& breathed- out…movably: moved: *re-cruited re-burned c®ooked*:

<Hostaged: to: fortune:

>Ex-changed…

<Help? Pay for advice: *list*:Depreciation! Credit?

>Bail-out?

<Bankrupt? Nation? Basics-required:restricted:: simplified independent-advice war-*orphans'* charging model *specific* one-off inherit pension-*portfolio* managed-fees:

>Fixed-retainer or: percentage-fee?

<For *larger*-amounts:*less transaction: fee-deal feder(e)al through home & small-business & personal-credit:*

on-screen bundled-up again: obliterating: traceable credit &: mortgages & un-paid-loans: swapping: send-to: then: delete: *deleting:*

>Homes:furniture: even-food…*even?*

<Evenly

spread…across Peoples' lives…

>Every-Ones? Not-possible:

<Why-not?

>Does not-compute:

<Do::*for one to make another must-lose or: de-value over time…*

WF4.159.

>The-Market: lists:of *lists:delete*...

The-Banker taken a-back:

Beneath-what were actually Gold-Gilt Bold CAPITAL-type captiontopping: & a clearly no longer tumultuous exchange Stock=Market recalled: The-Banker gradually & all too quickly: & suddenly & readily now recalling: implicitly getting-now: the pitiful irony of the newspaper headline:

WORLD MARKETS IN TURMOIL!

& the photograph below: Taken: without permission: who would be-*asked un-basked masked*...?

For: permission?

To the-Banker: now again: forcibly revealed: for the first-#time: by the-Clerk: perhaps: notoriously: not-only into short-term memory: but now also into open-consciousness:

Denied: as of this morning: Awakening as in a pent-up fury raging: invoked from the vestiges of the evening-prior:

'A phoenix to rise out of the *ashes*:' speech-bubbled: spoken out-loud:

Trimmed-wings is what the-Clerk thought:

'Business-as-usual?'

Looking out of the stilled moving-window:

'Business-as-usual: There is to be a Declaration this morning: by midday: Inter-national meantime:'

'Crow(n)ing-colonial…' *sanctioning Imperious-Independence...Gold-Sovereign fought-over freedom yet short< of the-markets...>*

'This-will stabilise the-markets…'

'At some-lower-rate: Others' automatically-*Higher*:'

'&: & that-is: the-thing! What 'We' will do is simply re-align currencies:::::…' the-Clerk interrupted: as if boring into the brain of the other as if to satisfy some lust or: hidden inbuilt-hatred avoidable as un-avoidable as both even as both an idle-interlocutor:

"We'? Same-thing 50/50? To: another relatively higher-point! You got it!'

'No: You got it:'

'&/or start all-over again? At: *some*-sum lower-point? You

give me the-nod on prices of one thing&another: & I-will: do the rest: get-me?

‘Fis(T/t)©ally speaking?’

‘Now then: those-debts: who they with?'

'*Errr*: you?"

'O:K: Right here: right now…’ *as issuing some or:atory usuryies’ declarative:*

Without clue of real-implication:

'Known? Collateral-damage? Un-intentional consequences:’

‘*Like*: honestyies’ politician-priests…’

‘If there were such a thing…’ *un-real time ready to be barracked self-deprecating & yet: as anyone appreciating of themselves promising deceiving of:* them-*selves*:

Implied de-preciation if any ap/p:reciation of the-other:

With the opportunity presented as an explanation of the rise to glorification: yet also thereby pre-emptive fall from grace:

Al(l)be-it temporarily:

‘*Bust-ups* break-outs:…’#

'Boom!!!'

Controversyies' sell-news…makes opinion-edit-ion…

As in current circumstances: as currency-account: as simplicity-Its'elf: &with: which/what 'It' would all be resolved today:

'Verifiable?'

'Falsifiable?'

'Bankers' Clerks' con.*fidence*…' heartened hand-pyramid:

'Secular-Politicians' Priestly-munitions…'

'Pre-monition: *(s)peculation…*'

'The-warnings given…'

'*Almost*…pro-phetic tricking-*normalityies*' immunityies' eliminating dis-informations…'

'Taken: Too-late: For that:'

'Warnings? Unheeded?'

‘After the event!’ &/*that* Front-page! That nevertheless now could only now be seen from the-Clerks’ supposed & likely derisive: & probably gloating: satirical perspective:

Once the side-panels rapidly absorbed: concerning the latest sports & business-media strategic celebrity-star photo of stage & screen politico-religious inoculating:

‘Keeping-up with the-markets…’ manoeuvring man-aging to outman-oeuvre competing strategyies’ tho’ never certain made to seem certain natural selection eliminating one over the-other…’ *shrieking-cheating monkeys’ scenario dis-traction* acting-bad/good *deep*-fakeryies’ lure-trap:

‘Keep-up with the…’

‘Neighbours’ World: Not-Paradise it seems…’ seen

through theft: & violence: on TV:

> *Status-Obesityies’ strategic-warnings’ fluffed: plucked: personal-value: emotional-distress:*
>
> *In a consumer-haze blazing marketing-characteristics: gentlerough capitalism-socialism shared-sharks’ circling*

the flotation-tank calming propitious-publicityies' canary in a cage:

Of the photogenic in-crowd the it-crowd & for the crowd-of: passengers generally-un-attainable:

Un-obtainable: & therefore to be utterly-loathed: or: loved: in equal un-equal measure:

Perhaps: as well as envied for their art or: wealth: or: both: & thus taken a part-of:

Most alarming of all the guileless: seemingly-misguided: trusted bought-newspaper: Now the even more incongruously: & mischief-making paradox-inducing intent: of a supposed-ally: notEnemy: anyway: not-yet: anyway:

The Tycoon-proprietor: manipulating Media-Mogul magnate-

0ligarchyies' empirical pseudo-economist wheeler-dealer: & owner:

With-whom: Banking:

'Gold&Golf' *may have been shared interests & at least & a singularly-shared bad literary-joke:*

Laughing together

Not-laughing together:

'This *little*-Turbulence…'

'With influence:' *still marking cards: making-detergent soap:*

or: string-balls:

Media-Empire vehicle whatever it was it mattered not:

Although 'It' did:

Truth as Lies: Lies as Truth…no-Truth anyway always shifty shifting goal-posts betrayer betraying even spiteful little-threat whenever not-making-out…

'It's what they leave out…' at the end of the day: when pushcomes-to-shove: no-one is or: ever was your-Ally: -even: your friend: not-even your-family:

Bailed-out: Bailing-out from the false-accounting phonetapping mess:

From: Power: corruption & lies…rate-setting: premium payment protection-racket:

Perhaps before anyone had tumbled…tumbled-in could have at least perhaps seen-it coming:

Could-have: perhaps should-have: acted with even-handed propriety: perhaps?

WF4.166.

Acting: with assumed-impunity: & as-usual uneven impropriety: summonsed-up & convinced & therefore convicted: in- their absence-of-wit:The- Editorial Traitors!
The Public: Closing-in: Closing-in:

'Closed-them down! I would!'

& closed-down the print-run down deliberately stopped the newspaper & the train-company from delivering:

'For-Free!'

Then:

'No more Well Fare Social-Securityies' No-more H&-

outs?!' let-slip:

'No more Bail-outs!'

'By & For whom?'

'The-Works:'

'The-Works?'

'**Rational Equitable**:'

> ***Rational Equitable:***

<Stores: Stocks: Goods&Services'

>Logistics'…

<Bread&Bandages' …

> Wheat & Weapons' silos docksides & runways…

<Military:

radio-equipment:*opening*:Battleships? Tanks?

<Militia-Soldiers' Poor-Boots on the ground…

Non-lethal:*supporting*:

>No-Fly-zone: then: destroying the

whole armaments' industries:

'Go where the clever-money is…'

Connecting:*connected…*

<Aircraft?: Tourism?

<Business-class:

> Freight? Military?

<Family? Too? To?'

>To: Debit-Credit Holiday!

Until things get back to normal: better: improve: -get-worse:

Both:

One: not-connected: re:

:connecting:disconnected:re-directing:

<>Desktop: *we are sorry that you are not-able to:your connection has -worked properly:*go- online to find a solution to this problem?: y/n:

>OK? Y/N: *yes/no*?

<No?

>Yes?:*we are sorry that you are not-able to:your connection has -worked properly:*go- online to fix this problem…fixing?:*click:*

Double-click:fixed: *fixing:*

<Factional…fictional…*almost* the-Party President-Sovereign…

>*Protracted*-Capital:

<Value/Risk: N/n:deposit/investment covered:

>Utilising-maximum:initial-payment…

<Free-Trade freeing-up Capita-*profit*...

>Freight-flight fight-*feint…*

massive-violence to the-engineering & on top of that: economic infra-structure risk-cheated public-private infrastructure sharing between countryies to countryies' place & people to people populations & actual-goods & buildings routes & ways:

>To establish perpetual-growth in-proportion to inheritance & wealth taken as unearthed…

<Un-earned?

'Destroying-Cityies'…Genocidal let me tell you something: You don't have to work hard to be rich: Figure that out…'#

'Call-out whole populations'…'

'Not your customer-base?'

'Not any-more terrorist home-base rule…beyond your wildest dreams!'

'Or: nightmares eh? Kill the competition?'

'I won't share this with anyone else: If I: shared there would be no point would there? Confidential insider get-me? No-leaks. If everyone knew about this? Who worked in restaurant hotel factory stores &/or: hospital there'd be no-one to work in restaurant hotel factory stores or: hospital would there? If there were none poorer than-us to spend their *hard*-earned wages week in week out: we'd all go broke!'

'Others have-to: work-poor for our-*wealth* to be worth anything!'

Pragmatic- ideologue! Ethnolinguistically gender & ability driven: strategic- falsely promoted tactics using history as: Clash-of-Civilisations:

'Not given-in to murder or: suicide…'

'Shop4Weapons?'

'Why not? Promote change for the better!'

'Tragically:'

'Pan-demic…'

'Laboratory-tested Research & Design Costs tax-free…expansive ex-pensive…'

'Price: Production:Promotion:Blown-up! Start-again…'

'Well done! *Sorry*:for selling-weapons of mass-destruction destroying by mass-war re-arming profit re-building a peaceful future until the next-one?'

'Always a next-one…'

'Sorry for getting-*caught*…'

'Not Me! Check-it!'

'I will:'

*

Steel-girders: & glass: The future: bringing out the past: from s& & rock: water & wind & gas an oil: *fractious*…

'For-War?'

'4-Good?'

WF4.172.

'Evil: Vile vial:'

'Everything in between…not-wanting to *Lose*: any of it!'

'On-*Fiscal*-Security?'

'Or?'

'Military-Security: *Beat* them down! No-business operates on

Real-economy terms: you must know that?'

'False-figures…'

'False-flags…'

'Rather than on simply:'

'*Pure*-monetary terms?'

'Interest rate losses adding to economy authorityies' de-

flating…' *take the-heat out-of: civil: cost-cutting governmental-service(s) re-entrenching private- public poverty-gap to: protect-private interest-familyies' fund-funded of the: very-rich with: in-heritance ploy pension-wealth exclude tax-raising & necessary to unnecessarily spend-on: people as economic objects subjects cut doesn't matter who or: what-on:*

'Government-Banks' in-federated in-corporate real-markets:

list: NN/nn::'

'Real Goods: What 'We' Will do: is simply re-align currencies…'

'Will '*We*'?'

'In-contestably:' *stabilise the-Global-markets at some lowerpoint & carry-on:Everything will start moving:Again: Universal finger-counting games on paper:*

The-Clerk looked-up:

'On-screen? Serious numbers! I don't usually ask twice: but do You want to take-a cut-in the Recovery eh? Cannot lose? Be in on the next Big-**Boom!!** Bang!'

'Basic commodities?'

'Rare *Metal*s?'

'**Food&Furniture**?'#

'There is more: in: Utilityies' **Oil&Gas**…' *under them-*there *desert-rocks' ocean-waters' past: passed-generations:* dinosaur-forests…dinosaurs'…life! Us! Fracking-Hells!'

‘*Generating*-Energy: Everyone needs…’

‘Plastic…’

‘Explosive:…’

‘<u>Uranium</u>? <u>Plutonium</u>?’

‘Burning-Re-sources Waste4Energyies’ against free wind-water-solar:…’

‘<u>*Polonium*</u>:<u>Industrial</u>: or: <u>Military</u>-use?’

'<u>Business</u>?'

'Loan: To be *had*?’

‘Strip-Mining minerals from The Earth…’

‘Seen from Space? Eh?’

‘Satellites & Solar-panels perhaps?’

‘Who knows? Exciting-*possibilities’ as we-do:-think we have to be persuaded:*

Know what I mean?

Threat?

‘Just: A simple '<u>Yes</u>’ is all 'We’ need…’

WF4.175.

‘Who doesn’t?’

‘For a *comfortable*-Peace?’

'Piece? Of What?’

‘@*Never*:say: Never!’

'*What? Why-not?’*

‘Uncomfortable with War: then?'

‘That is war?’

‘Isn't it?’

‘Why would you not-w*ant* Peace?’

‘Like we had before *this*?'

'*This*-time?’

‘Last-Time::’

‘Can-not: have *the*-same-again: ever?’

‘Every-time: is different?’

‘Of-course: *Virtually*…preserved…populations…’

'By MAD-ness! Mutually Assisted Destruction:’

'Assured?'

'Nu-Clear Insured?'

'You think you are…'

'No? Know (Y)Our…breaking-point:' *snapped! broken into-pieces micro-waved radiated-goodness…turned to: fear turned to: anger:*

'The-Whole-Thing…collapsed! Whether-*designed* to or: not-to:with Catastrophic-damage:for-*some*:
Ful(l)some: Co-Lateral: Ig(s)nored: Not-All: See?'

'Cannot-be?'

'Again?'

'Yet?'

*

Suburban-edges: trimmed-hedges: overgrown woods: & peeling whitewash walls: Compound 3 or: 4 storied building: & alongside creosoted-fences: before the graffiti-walled enclosed-ditch: between poplar & ash-growing: pastures: & harvested-fields: By the railway=track…*looking*-out:

‘Agri-Culture…cattle-feeding pig&sheep chicken-factories…’

‘Killing-fields: ground-burst accidental air-bursts de-liberated

on: *killed hundreds of thousands more hundreds of thousands since*

with viral cyber-disease cancer birth-defects as many civilians as get killed

now against humanitarian rules of wars broken-brokered broken-again today…’

‘For: harvest wheat&cattle-meat to: steal:-’

'The-City…Business as Usual:’

‘So: Stupid! Damn-lies: re-peated end-lessly…’

'Until now:’

‘It was all going so well:’

'Ostrich!’

‘Head in the sands of time…’

'So you knew?'

'What? Duck in the water! of course: Boarding-Statistics…'

Weather-reports as now un-reliable as un-predictable as each-other…without proper-analysis…confidence…

($)lacking fixtures&fittings…

'See that is it…that is what You work with:'

'Bonus! To work for IT now: Banks' Government:' statistical…*interpretation*…used:

'True or: False…' messaged:

'Anything in-between:'

'How you like it:'

'Crackdown on cheating corruption-fraud! Tax evasion?' *Avoiding friendly-fire: financially…sue for accidental-damage de-claiming!*

'Being bombed-out!'

‘Red Barbarian at the gate!’

‘Honest Green Giant?’

‘Locked-out: Making-size&re-sources count!’

‘Insider-Hulk?! Media *Bluey*-Meanie:’

‘Alright: Don’t be-*stupid*:’

Turned-away: & down into the-screen: playing: *the*-Game:

‘*Economic*-BRIC-A-Brac Bank=BLOC(K)s’…’

‘…Expediencyies’…pragmatism: Fair?’

‘The Brick-*value* … ‘ changed-*charged*…

‘Brick-*Bat*:?’

seen:

>Y/N?::

<Y! Development-Bank:

➤ Infra-structure: building: employing:

& employing:Government-Licencing::

con.tact:::cont®acts::::

<Contact: buying-&-selling always:

all-ways!

>The Great-Game!: Play!

'The-*Gambler* bets on what they *believe* may -happen: won't necessarily happen:'

'Taken leave of their good-senses in analysis that others' do not-know: once-known cannot un-know are -*meant* to know:'

'Customer-Clients'Club?'#

'Share-holders? The-People! Are - *meant* to know!'

*hushhush:*cl&estine:*covert*:

'Who's backing who is to-Live?'

'Lives. **Food&Drink**: & the **Chairs&Tables** of all those G*'s*

of the:'

'Global-7's…eights' nines' & 10's…'

'There are only individuals: & families playing-the-tables:'

O Dictatorship-authoritarian Militaryies vs Para-Military oiling the wheels…

‘Other-wise?’

‘World-Food programme to-*understand*: Business…’

‘With an air of fulfilled destiny!’

denying lying...laying waste moral ineptitude smuggling weapons for food drying-up ending-up one-sided in-League the-little league other-others’ enemies...

<Government-Bonded bound-Corporation(s): *listing*:

‘Get-in *early*:’

‘International-Conference:…’

‘In-sider info®mation…’

‘Treatyies’ pro-tec(h:)(t)ion…’

‘Done-dealing?’

‘Could not-stop ourselves: could we? ‘It’: was just: too-Good! To be-True!’

‘The-Truth? Oil-Gold: Game-over: Enviably too-Big to Fail:’

‘The rest of Us?’

'Too small to survive?'

'Society?'

'Politics of Envy?'

'You too?' *envied* all the same:

'Arguably:to Bad to Fail:'

"'Too-Bad to fail?'

'Only winning-bids now…'

'All caught: dead or: alive…' *if -toppled already: those who top-themselves: through the roof: : believing-nothing but themselves could top-that…*

Top-Hat! Assuming-Absolution with Absolute-Power!
Palace-

Power!

'Owing?'

'Ow(nnn)ing?'

<NNN:

Call-themselves Plutocratic-si(g)nology necrologyies…loud-noise mob-action: public gr&eur: publicly anonymous self-isolators:

WF4.183.

>Selfers: Sell no-*choice* option: Neutrality compromised: or: not: Integrated: Wireless re-charging *connection*:

Aside: On-screen-risk-monitor: *pressing-key*:

>In &:

<Out:

>Import /Export::N/n:

>N/n?

<n/N: Export /Import: in the middle-North & Southern islands & continents':

>Whole countries!

<Smaller & larger:

>Federations: financials…

under>funded-aid…

<Global: From Africa&Arabia to Israel & Egypt back to *Babylon*: Iraq to Iran…

> Carthage-Rome Italy2Tunisia Sudan Syria to Afghanistan around the *virtual*-virtuous equator…*quaking*...

>Pakistan India Russia China Africa challenging military-support for Indonesia&Japan: The-Koreas…

<Money-Infra-structure Australasia:

>Chile: Peru Argentina Brazil Venezuela Mexico:

>The *USofA:* Canada:

< Climate-Culture of nu-clear financial-*Fear*! Russia Now!

back-to Africa & the near-far & middle-East: Europe:&

the-North:

<To the-Arctic-*circle* of-course: : new gas & oil there:

magnetic-north: : South-Antarctica: *southern-cross shown:* north-star

rising east-west luminaries in their own lunchtimes out-*shining*

>Inner:& Outer-Space!

<The-Globe! on-screen spun once more: East & West:

North: & South: : from-where? *Graffiti-wall: cartoons: symbols miss-represented-youth: shot: beaten & tortured outpourings of playful-Rage!*

Scaring into sub-mission…

Not knowing what the future would hold:

Set-fire to homes: schools: nurseries: brothels&casino fiscal gambling-dens:

Bombed border-blockade: by sea & mountainous land river & air: home in-vasion:

>Until the-dues Tax/Tariff: *is paid*:

<Dues are Paid? How?

>Public-Subsidyies' Energy-Charter Act in Good-Faith: Ha!! Decisions: good&bad for: Free-Trade Aid! By any other name!

Fraudulent:

< Government-Corporate Corrupt: Bail-Bonded-out…

>Timing: is everything: T-minus: plus: added: T1-2:

<Non-Governmental-Organisation: *innovating* driving-golden-ticket golf-ball allowance-of: the-future in&out:…

>As?

the overbearingly righteous murderous moment: wildly off beam bean-counters' ...

Wide of the mark:

> Monopolyies' Ma®king necessity ideologically…

& Practical suggestions please to get us out of this Stagnation! toadying obsequiousness! Fawning-flattery! Sycophancy-Succession!

<Hedge! HEJ Health Education Justice…

> Just-Ice! Freeze: To buy-back @the@The-People@This morning in Geneva there is to be an announcement-of: The International Conference on Monetary Compliance (ICMC):

>St&@****-Off! *Phoney@*War!

<****+War: How much to borrow? Amount?

>Anything!

<Paranoid!

>Unreasonable! What is Reasonable?

Second-*C*lick: Accountancy (workings): NNN (a number):

Third *C*lick: clicked on & thought *decimating social- local economy community-industry: spelled-out:*

<Energy dec.im(it)ating social-local economy community industrial-imperious cultural-colon(den)ialism: ex-colonial **black-***fo(n)ot* colonising colonists' countries of origin no-where…

>Through force of law eliminate peoples'

cult.u/r(e)allyies' possess-ions' live-l(*i*)hood… *sub-*

jugated relatively imp-overished tran(s)ported paid-

for:

<But what choice did We have? Sell Sell Sell! like the

- Supermarket! Market-Domination! obsess-

i/v(e)it(y)ies'

< Buy! Buy! Buy! Shopping-Trolley Therapy Wars!' critical *customer caught in the middle buy what you can sell what you can't credit payments be your own thieving banker-breaking rules'o'fiscal distribu(t)(e)ion O'wealth dictat. cost-price of: wages/salaries=goods/services awareness don't get caught by corruptors corrupting disloyal lawyers only-just doing their thing we selling sales three short steps commission interest want then need bonus-deposit subscription tied-in: hold-out the cashcard take-the: cash-card dis-appear chaser-now being chased-to: where the bla(g)h-blo(ck)g: scam spam scan…bonus-begins…*

Competitive-Tarriff/Free-Trade=Free-Labour=Servant-Slave Trading…

Capital Opportunity-Costs=*mean*(s)o'production+Techno.tools'

{(p)lan(d)(n)ed.}: Control-Command Communal-Economyies'

'To: get: r(i)ch-qu(*i*)ck=educate: make-work: hard(errrr?)!'

poorest-worker work-hard too-to: workless exploited too-slowly

eats away...sleep-dream die for: the-Local/Global market &

then: without further re-course:

'*Another* global-failure: fiscal-politically...

'RE-warded:'

'Peoples' Pal(l)-ace Police-Pro-tected:...'

'Militarily...specialising-in: dependencyies' of: other(s):'

<<u>Select</u>::*extra*-judicial execution assassination: rebels freedom-fighters terrorists: in the-field:

> Colonial-capturing traitor tried as terrorist as prisoners invasion occupy settled currencyies' captured settlement-enclosures en-hanced lanced interrogation technique:

<Interrogator: *consistent pattern-of-torture discriminating & as indicating-orders:*

> Inequalityies' Heirarchyies' Natural:

<From the Big-Top Safe-*haven*:

>Punitive-Airstrike!

<Arm the-Population!

>Calls for-Country-list: *list*: ::

<Vote-Census: *list*...

>Differential producer-*consumer*...

*

Crisis-*Capitalism*…Tragedy of the Commons'…

<Differential meaning Rich & Poor: multi-relativist…

> Plutocratical…*diversity*: actually make anything but Money and miser-able lives of others?

<Singular-Social-*ideologyies'*? You want that?

> Not-too-much povertyies' enough pay to get-by as imprisoned consumers want what we give them and be glad.

necro-politic effect...

WF4.190.

Difference deferred deferential & dis-placing:

>With constant–innovation:capital & labour-time in contradiction of the-*subjective*:

< Objective: : Profit: : T1: make®: T2: tran(s)porter: : T3: tax-ideology *idol*atryies' *icono'clasm*: *margins* mending N/n producer/consumer: World: goes' round&round…space/time place-time all of Y(Our) places times altering every moment seconded costed-price market-place trip-lic(k)ate copies' o®(i)ffic(e)(*i*)al(l)-stamped: fending-off the *Chaos* that inevitably *exists* & is the only *truth*-perhaps:

'Terrorist regulatory fiscal-fanatical *devils*' fantastical nihilistic-gods&murderous social-suicid(e)ALL! Oligarch-Elite oppositions: & *de-pendencies:*:

<Victory!

not-extirpation but *emergence*:

>Money used as(s):*entice*ment turning people into *Zombies'* Voodoo-Obeyahhhhh!!!!!!!!!!!

'Its' *happening* now!'

*

WF4.191.

Hacked to bits: With giant flaming swords: or: blasted into the air:

By powerful magic: League of Legends: protection from harm doing harm competitive tempers tamed by abuse dealt with by the protagonists & by definition also antagonist behavioural-profiles: innocence/guilt prescribed proscribed inter-acting::run-high or: lowcurses insults de-rogating…

<Opponents::& Allies: *filleting* the-regulars: Drunk-

Trolls&Fun-Junkies:

> Making-it all up as we go changing tunes' switching

sides…

*

Tribunal: *aggregating bad-behaviour chat-logs chastened chastising bubbles of speech floating to the-top…*

Table-forum un-chaired file-shared: open-discussion: chaired: de-layed for: ever & quickly closed:

<Shut-down deal? Stay-Open? Which would you prefer?

>Advise:

be-careful: mis-takes happen: we cannot stop every disaster mis-steps say sorry and move-on up:

WF4.192.

*Victims'... violation claimed as Perps: Perps as Victims' Villains egregious judged offending doing bad things for the right reasons...right for the wrong reasons banned-for: good&ever/or: for a time-out reparation-*period*: set by the agreeing players to the rules this time & how they will be interpreted meted-out metred & dealt-with:*

'Kicked-down the-Road: All-way(s)…old&older

new&newer social-democratic standards to be met…'

'Lawyers' well-fare meaning & in-effective eventually after the immediate-*attack*: in-affective: not taken as well-meaning: even-if: even ever clearly understood: simple messages advertising *ad:vising…*'

'Getting people to buy our products against their own best-sense: competition Sense of Worth Life-Value…' status-*envying* campaign-*leaflet campaign:or TV in(ter(n)-ception ad.vertising impossibly positively campaigning...*

'A-*Vert…*'

'*Green*-washing machine-tech. laundering…'

'They will never agree:'

'They are like governments…cannibals eating their

own…'

'Shit! Throttled at birth…'

'Attempting to eradicate…'

'Ourselves 'We' don't make anything remember?'

'Except ourselves'…'

'Money? To: eat? breath?'

'To: educate?'

'Violence getting closer…'

'Political-Economic aspirations get rich quick…'

killing…

'Blood-cur(d)ling threat…'

'Gang-Warfare: Abstracting: Br&names &logo-on: leisure&re-creation:…'

as well as substantive-*existence*:…

'No problem:'

'Correct:'

'True? Fail: *They* buy from the companies we own:

medicals to heavy-weapons:

'We' sell *them* medicals to cover lost-weaponryies all-over the last continent to get their-own:...'

'Sunk-treasure debts the same as any other: taken-by some former colonialist classic-competitive market-place: exchanging-value: war-weighed in our favour: of course! Win-Win!'

'Score-draw?'

'Equality? not-or(e):...'

'Status-quo? Elite-Establishment...'#

'Here to stay? All-good: always...Famil(t)yies' *schooled...*'

'Sexual-Psycho. abuses...'

on-line & fronted-by official-*forces*'...'

'As long as no-one else notices: eh?'

'Their-People:'

'Or ours?'

WF4.195.

Up-vote or: down-vote: incumbent-posts & position: on a 4D map & working mechanisms that allow: societal-norms (e)mergent on-line: city-countryies' communities:

'Shaping our-communities:

'Sharing-in:…

'Inevitably *anyway:*'

'Of-course: Judge & Jury every-Mo. *meant…*'

'Afterwards: Only One-Decision: That is all 'It' takes:'

'Maybe: Many others:'

''We' gotta be-nice to too?'

'Of-course.'

<Secular-Ideological Monetarist/Communist Theo-cratic/ un-Diplomatic*: pressure: prime-pumping sub.(s)-money:*

>Allies: list:*list:::*

< Energyies' Enemies: list:*list:*

We all got them: haven't we?: list:

Sensitive in(*side*)&out(side):

Rippling: to&fro:

Up&down&along: & backward: & forth: in>machines: <created by ourselves: on road: & rail: into *the*-space:

Magus-aegis anti-ballistic agues not-doing atmosphere leaving satellite cyber TV strike: & eliminating counter-missile in: Space:::sophisticated counter- measures:
decoy-satellite:long-range missile:-

<But sooner: &/vortex.t-later?

>If you've got them: Nuclear-product World-Domination!

< Gold-Gas&Oil!

>Warheads?

<So what? Cyber-securityies'…*un*-done:

Computer-consoling…remote-control robotic auto-intel:

to work on the deep-sea harbour:

To *placate* the water: *spirits* & *Slave*-on taken to an *invisible*-

Plantation:

Commodity *fetish*:

Fearing victim & victor:

Pious-death

Ceremonial-passed:

'The-*Magician's Trick* I like best:'

'The-Sorcerer:' engendering puzzlement:

'Witching…'

'Like some dis($)-interested Economist-Scientist!'

'Murderous Nihilistic & Suicidal Devils!'

'Soldiering-on…'

'Soldiered sealed entombed:' *magic & wonder-working marked-occult:*

Riches: & rituals:::only::what about Liar:?

Laired? Snared...

Trapped in a cup-of-crap:

'Shit! of your *own* making!'

'These *Loans*: then? You signed for them agreed those didn't you?'

Lion-roars! When it gets Hungry! roaming:to: re-connecting:

<*Vanity*-Project: *protection…soars!*

The Banker-concluding:

'This morning in Geneva there is to be an announcement of the International Conference on Monetary Compliance (ICMC): There is to be a shared-Protocol: This is expected to stabilise major-Global currencies: & exchange-rates at some lower-rate: to boost-confidence in the banking-System & World-trade again:'

‘’We’ shall see:’

>Select: *gaming*:Long-term R/Evolution 4G: for WarFare4: Modern Gr& Armies vs Allied Coalitions Continental Blockade (Cannon Rifle)/ World Wars (Machine-Gun anti-tank Aircraft): Modern-Contemporary World-Wars:Inter-Continental Civil-War(s)…

Inter-Continental-CivilWar/Countries’ Civil-war Ballistic Missile Nuclear Warhead Satellite in Space recent history: Modern-Contemporary: Chemical Biological:Nu-*clear:*

Global-power vs: failed Rogue-terror Trade-State: fogging the outlook from the air…to the ground:

‘NO!oooooooooo!!!…’

'Drone-ON!’ steered from someway distant airdrome:paired deskissuing manoeuvrings:orders: to kill: to hold-back for more information: the-Clerk: turned-away: looked-out again: & back through the reflection on-screen:

<Active-search…>& looked down into the Game:

>Play y/n?:Y…& now resuming:

<Game-play:…

lost against the once more hushed hubbub separately now again transparently looking seeing straight-through moving…movedalong:through differently seen scene: improvised-*accompaniment* musical or: otherwise improvised:anyway:

Played-out: as a workplace journeying as with some holidayfiction now:

The-Clerk re-opening:

>Currency exchange: list:R/e:N/n:

<Buy Money-for-Money-*at*:

>Exchange-rate in World-reserve & exchange currencies: R\e:/list:… US/Australia/Canadian Dollar/Yuan-*Mindi Yen*/Sterling*silver* Gold-R&/new-Ruble/new-Dinar/ convertible-Peso/ Rea & Rupee: Shekel/R(i)yal…Euro:

for-bearance to the holder bearing of your:

>Select-one: other-currency only at…

<Currency-conveyance converting: R/e:/any…

other:?:N/n:*advantageous*-rate::select: your-currency::R\e…N/nn:& another(s)…: (to which all others pertain with some exceptional mutuals'& internal-markets'…:

<Credit-Debit: Union…

> Economic-Zone: *list…5/6 serious slight* surprise or: Shock -Awe…yet: on the back of the Real-economy (s)elected…the real-thing?

>Linked smaller currencies to larger…

<Street & market-place Markets:trading:continues…

>The-Global situation:

Money-economy/Real-Economy: Your=*money* economy & *real*-Economy…*things*:& counting Nnnn:

Time: Hh/mm/ss/6:00…A:M: World-Time:12:00:minus:

The-radio with sorted & often scant news:

Messages like:

‘Political-propag&a news seemingly irrelevant:’ & …al(l)=*most* in-comprehensible:’

Anyway-all

As Citizen-Reporter: re-porting:

): You may choose from a limited: Bank-set::

<Your-own: Economic-zone interest-rates outgoings & earnings on savings…& debts:n/N:

(: Like-nepotistic:who you know:like who you are royally married-to? specific-allyies…

<Loans you have made to Family & Friends:

>Supervision of Fraud & recklessness: wrecking-ball…

<Crash! & as lender of last resort to any friends & family who may require assistance & for who you are responsible for::

>To-whom you owe a Duty-of-Care or: couldn’t care-less…

<As well as Yourself

>Or not-at-all! Buy into Commodities then:

<N?::

Search: Global Market:Analysis: clicked &:yet another-set of graphs & charts:broad-cas(t)ing:

>Crop-report figures coming-in…N/n…

<Side-bet! Insurance claim-settled to be settled?
>Compensation-culture!

< &: Hustle-loans mortgaged death-gauged pledged against properties & Businesses…paid-off & defaults higher/lower: in Credit/Deficit: N/n… N/n to spend on what? With-what?

>Not: What then?

<The weight of Popular Opinion:

The Un-stoppable Train to Consensus-Cityies'

<u>True</u> *believers*:

Traditional Ideation-holders…in various colours & message-board reenforcing…*information*: *shared*-Belief all-different place/time more than one-other self-righteousness…

< Battle(s)! Life! War! Fair!!!

>*What is that? Sharing…*

<Enough through:

>*Hysteria-Mass liquid withdrawal un-met by moonlight…*

Looking-up again: the-Clerk: to the-Banker: on the train: to the-City:

Peacetime-makers/Wartime workers

Public: Credit-Debt:

Double-dealing rhetoric:

>Public-face privately coldly ruthless:

Silent condoning: Loud con:damnations…

>Creating upping the-anti *rhetorical*-leaks:

<Virulent:

>Viral:

<We know:

*

Confrontation deliberately with the-West/East separatism re-pression at-Home: huge m&ate from the-People! Believe! *Terror*-transformer: massacre with Fear&Anger: revolt re-vulsion pro-pelling political- economic & media-pundits expert-citizen@per-citizen: re-porting:-

'Intercepting::'

on: video radiowavelength:

>Securitising- death assurance *secondary*-bet on how soon x-

dies:

<Worse-*coursing* effects market-*Triumphalism!*

>Stake-in the outcome:

<Pay & pricing communality civic society military con. tractors outsourced-War! Private-Public Partner-Ships Tanking…

- Farm-War(s)?

Marker: a-moral neutral-insensitive marketisation non-*judgmental*:

<Freely-queuing ability road-toll life-insurance mutual-financial:

>Food-Pay to-have children read cash incentive/free-

food:

<Confidence trust undermined morality no: of players taking-cut familial-securitised goods:

> Succession(s)-*Stolen:* children.

*

Reigning-agencies primary-instruments for achieving public-good:

<EveryDay behaviour:*belief-systems apolitical a-moral a-religious ethnic-ethic as if the future matters: nature-pollution pension-fairness here-&-now:*

think-tank the Centre for Social-Justice political think-tanks deserve *their* charitable-status glossed-over pay-need to take particular care when publishing research that contains recommendations of a political nature commissioning legal advice on regulator carelessness approach to regulating political think tanks particularly those who don't disclose their sanctioned knight in shining-silver golden solar-armour bronzed dough-nors…

>*Fix the Future! Olympian!*

*Inform yourself! Today! prices empirical pragmatic value-neutral science utilitarian theory of value: lasting will go up: why?in: centive need...then...greed...*global-optimal sol.(u)(t)ion(s):

< Industrial(m)isa(t)ion: *up-grade product profit create constantly upgrading need for good discover new means through competition material limits of endless-growth: propag&a(t)(e): advertising personal-victoryies' could be you!*

But…isn't:

Haven't worked hard-enough to get here drop-a-rung or: too-this: is: a hereditary-stake state-peerage: gone-rogue…cit.(i)zen den(i)zen…

>Utilitarian-economic model:-1-2player 3+multi-player:

Instinctive non-market free-market medical service free/cheap/reasonable responsibility professional personal duty of care housework/bonding boarding-family inheritance stock-market grizzled-guru was only-ever lucky with wealth-play:

<Elections::*connecting: fixed eventually all other parts of the Ancient-l& & L&:beyond unseen as yet from:*

the-wealthiest campaign is the one most likely to win…only if you play your cards before layabout betting-on:

Business-Centre:

Name: **The: Rational-Equitable**:

>Your-Business-Centre::

<*Vanity-project!* Man(i)pulating?

>How-so?

<The-City named after you: The currency named after your City:Your-Town… >**Equitable-**

Town::

>**Rational-City**?:

<**Reasonable-Village&%**?

>&-***Currency***::*opening*::

< **Rational-City:** O:K?:

Rational-Equitables: **R/e**:'s':

<**Town & Country**:**E/rrrr…**

>***Inter-National***:

<**Continental**:**Global R/e**:Nn:

Out by the airport…appeared prompted by-*clicking*:

<**Building**-*materials:* **Food&Furniture**...**Media?**

>...& Luxuries:: item's...including: Your Businesscentre:...the-Bank of You:how many floors? (give a number up to 100) & a number-given:

>Nnn...

The-Clerk entered another number: by speaking: saying the number word: flashed on-screen & clicked:

<Nnnn:Loan?:Nnnn:Agreed...dropped-in in a shower of coinage & paper-notes & the-Banker photo-caricature cut-&-pasted from::

>Application(s):...*behind re-enforced protective-glass walls fluttering down the screens now:at the-Top on the top: from the top inside:the-Banker: aviator-avatar sat behind mahogany-varnished desk:-table showered: with gold & silver...spouted from & falling over-a:><World-map: less-trod:* carpeted shades of black & white-light-brown & yellow & green deep blue seats: seas & ocean cloud: above: & beneath: bordering a blazing red-Sun:

Looking-out: & in: onto & through-out modernist strangelyangled sheet-light colour-stained glass: & plastic-panel: see-through from ceiling to floor:

Looking-over: a bustling ancient marketplace: fruit&vegetables livestock trading-posts outposts stalls set-out within be-low or: without that which could -physically be brought-to market:

Due to bulk-mass: type & value…in-Transit or: still-in: the-*ground*:

On-the-ground: somewhere elsewhere & never to reach here at all but *boarded-out* in letters & numbers in-full: … hidden: or: chalked-up & under-the:-: cast *wrought*-iron frame: & steel-blue counter plastic-coated former-formed sulphurous plutonium-patterned sheet-topped tables gambling-houses: betting-shops&*public*-houses:on the: Train: as tea & coffee-shop bought full-size screened-sports&places-of: barter&banter: debt/debit left-handed righteous-equation:

Assets=liabilityies'&Equityis' owner-ship own-a-ship(s):

sunk-costs in-creases assets de-creasing liabilityies' equityies' owed-to:

A.N. Other:

Sport&Art: of re-pute: Commodityies' Good(s) lain-in…laid-in & on & over the lay-of-the-land: laid-down: planned-over panning-out: from…

Town &:Urban(*e*)-centre market-place courthouse over veg.etable & fruits of the Earth &…livestock market-place…

The-Banker/Clerk avatar-stepped-out through the window as a helicopter flew close-by:

Stepped-into: Nnn: floors-*up*

X/x-terior elevator glazed window-wall fitted-gated gilded–cage: to the underground basement car-park…

Out-driving:an extraordinarily: exorbitantly expensive-vehicle from *list*::the-full range: list: selected & clicked-on: the-now: *self-owned* now advertorial-character inside: seated: persuaded: cheated:intogears…transmission-automatic: *on the game-pad console: buttons & switches screeching-away between walls: & ramps: skidding-around to a:Halt:*

Taken-over: then: then around-&-out between buildings streetby-street through layer upon layer blocks-of-building(s'o'lar...

Buildings:ancient:& new:& buying & adding-to...added to all along the way...

Railway bridged underpass: river-banks &:

Estuary-Tunnel: through to the other-side: turning: turned: & cliff-edged overlooking-Water! Screeched: braked & spun-around again: hitting a key on the steering-wheel:

<No Credit! Best-time! **<u>GO!</u>**

>Debt/<u>Bet</u>-time!

<Speed-cameras:watch-out!

>Pay-up: re-fuse)al may cause:

<Re-fused?

>*Anger!*

In-red: In-blue:

<No: Offence:

>No-offence: Skint: This is what 'It' is: Go on the offensive!

<What for?!

>You're thinking of *driving the*-Car…Drive!

Washed-up?oN THE BEACh? bIEAK?

Down-river to the-City edges of Fielded Forest & Hill & Mountain…

>Build-first…ask questions later…on unclaimed-*swamp* inspite of anyone else before anyone else: Training & options' *mode…*

<This Time!…& at the Great-river lake: & scenic Oceanic:

From the cliff-topped taking-off over the water & turning far out inland & again: Alongside fields & irrigation-ditch to l&-afloat:
on swampland draining estuary basin…spinnaker windsail…out-again on the water onto peninsular-sea…mapping… loading…waiting…

Motor speedboat with increasing speed: plummeted plunged: & sunk submerged submarined: To avoid various-objects imperilledon: & in-the-water implied-Shark infested-waters blubberous…

Whale: Mackerel & Cod: Sardine shell-fish until there was nofish left: blown-up!

<Cleaning-up?

>The-Train?' >

<***The-Gleaner***? Get Me? Electric? Green-Hydro.

genius!!!

>You got it:If You want to bring in rich-investors & investment-in:

< Confidence

> Scientific-research::done::see? rased raised-*surfacing* & water-ski-ing wet-suited clad with the:

<Is that the…:

R\E *logo…taking-off gliding with wind-surfing balloon opening-up: & rising into the upper-atmosphere looking down over a countrytown tour aloft over-looking casually & without due regard then straightening-up…ready…re-turning towards the-City-airport executive-transformation performing:*

>*Helicopter-view*…H-Land:-*perfectly* exactly on the-built: **Business-centre**: roof-top's stretched out to the urban & suburban distance: In-between the factories & office-blocks:

<*Real*-estate::*beneficial*-owner: N/nnnnnnnn: in the clear-air…as commentary-spoken continued through headphones:text?/spoken:

>Choose?: text spoken:click's made over a ragged landing-over fields:& Farm: Factorial-buildings: *list*:

Factory or: *y/ou*®- own:

Home: or:

Businesses-Centre:

City-Bank:

the circuitous roads now heavy with cars lorries buses & coaches mechanised streets: Populated with identikit people of almost every personality-type & head & shape of every ethnic-race & apparent-creed & ideogram mixed:

<As long as there has been & is & there will be:

<**Food&Furniture** household-goods & materials for making: on the back of carts & trucks: lorries & coaches & cars:

On the concrete-built motorways container-juggernauts: into&-out of Village: Town: & to & from each: & the-City:

On the sea & land a-waiting at-dockside & harbour fishingvessels: ships & supervised controlled Hyper-tanker: & from the high-seas & Ocean waiting-off shore:

Sea-port passed the coastal & inland estuary river-Towns: list: already built-up: out-skirts: & back in-to: lights: lit-up:

The: Rational-Equitable:

tower building-up through riverway-lined embankment: canal & railway-track: Up: & along evermore & faster: building-checking maintaining- control by-braking: gradually>spinning-on a too-rapid action:

'The-Deal:' *lost*: On: to the next-above from satellite-dish

solar-panelled beaming-in below:

>**Country&Countries**: list: in the-*Cloud*…

the-lofty^*City*streets&buildings now: tra(i)n.sformed from bricks & mortar: tracks & (e)plan(e) pie-chart…

<Projected-costs (Blue) & Projected-earnings (Yellow):

>Business-Plan (*Green*): *hydro*-genic…

Balance-sheet (red/black): on screen like towers-building: *tumbling*:

& dropping: & rebuilt once more: only to fall:

<You: are safe within the **Black**-zone…stray into the *Green*zone & you are out-in-the-open…*heard...fuzzy found-footage...in blocks & relief red & black with green thread's & lines like the real hills beyond & blue: beyond the columns &*

row's:with a bright yellow sun: in a bright blue: in the sky: bright-clouds: 🌢Oh *Grey-*
Black*...*

<Danger-Red or:ANGE: *yellow...*

>City: Towns & countryside-Village…& hamlet…

tokens taken the place of the buildings & roadways green fields & trees digitally-transferring between & across spread-sheet & balance-sheet number & text-wrapped boxed & charted:graphicsmapping:where l&scape & livestock once were:outside & inside...& on the single wall flat-screen back in- **The Rational-Equitable** building:

<Access-denied! flashing-on & off…

>Your password code?:YyyyyXNnnn…

<:*re-cognised…*

>O:K: You are Trading: Private Limited Company: Trading under the name::

<***The Rational Equitable***: OK?

>OK?

<Rational u r classic-actor: acting to::maximise Personal & others' Economic-return-on-*Investment:*…

>*Your:* Budget for the-day:

On-screen: with Real-world up-dates:

<Real-time & Game-play-currency setting-up…

Not-budging:

>Tough-budgeting:

<No it's not!

it's a piece of piss…as long as there is enough demand to meet supply chains inter-linked with demand or: is it the other-way-around?

>Not-constant de-valuation of the currency?! Only not-inflationary…between…wages & prices usually…between high(s)&low(s):

<Monetary-goals: full-employment: *always* something to be done: paid-for:

>A Home of: you®-own: maximise people before profit:

maximising-interest: before: propertyies'...

< Ransom(e) hostage to Big-Business benefit-cost for:

>Pension-Insurance: *structural-demand&supply-chain: logistics a-voiding frictional-mismatch between choices...between employment&un-employment paid-for:*

<What choice is there? *Wages & prices at the shops: Payday-*

loan? for:

>Cost-price stability... dealing with conflicting interests across:

<Investments: (bets) taken-out on accredited interest rates:

>Evens/Odds...N/n to one: in Real-time flashed-up:

Time: YYYY/MM/D/Mx60...sx60...12:00 midday minus:

> NNnnnn...counting-down: or -up: whoever: what-way

you came-at IT at midday: from the past: from the- future...

<So set-out your bargaining counters: You!: set-out yours:

>Your bargaining chips:Nnnn…

to-gether the Merchant-Banker&accountant-Clerk checks the winner: &/or: there you go:

<Great Journey of Discovery… completed…continue?: Y/N?Y……from the:Dark-Ages to the Enlightenment…to the Spaceage…Now!: Denomination of Credits neutral one-to-one…amount?: Nnnnnnnnn…Your password:

<YyyyyXNnnn:

>Again?: YyyyyX Nnnn:Xxxxxxxy…

loading…re-colonising towns & villages with long-range guns contain&dominate: where only now non-humans lived&worked-to: death joining others & *almost*-destroying although that patently not-possible as roundly shown in figures: statistics: needed throughout the Ages…colonists/colonial-other *settling: leavers&re-mainers' re-t®ainers…running…*

continued…

Standard Oil Co. (Pablo Neruda, Canto General, 1940)

When the drill bored down toward the stony fissures and plunged its'

implacable intestine into the subterranean estates, and dead years, eyes of the ages, imprisoned plants' roots and scaly systems became strata of water, fire shot up through the tubes transformed into cold liquid, in the customs house of the heights, issuing from its world of sinister depth, it encountered a pale engineer and a title deed.

However; entangled the petroleum's arteries may be, however the layers may change their silent site and move their sovereignty amid the earth's bowels, when the fountain gushes its paraffin foliage,

Standard Oil arrived beforehand with its

checks and it guns,

with its governments and its prisoners.

Their obese emperors from New York are suave smiling assassins who buy

silk, nylon, cigars

petty tyrants and dictators.

They buy countries, people, seas, police, county councils, distant regions where the poor hoard their corn like misers their gold:

Standard Oil awakens them, clothes them in uniforms, designates which brother is the enemy the Paraguayan fights its war, and the

Bolivian wastes away in the jungle with its' machine-gun.

A President assassinated for a drop of petroleum, a million-acre mortgage, a swift execution on a morning mortal with light, petrified, a new prison camp for subversives,

in Patagonia, a betrayal, scattered shots beneath a petroliferous moon, a subtle change of ministers in the capital, a whisper like an oil

tide,

and zap, you'll see

how Standard Oil's letters shine above the clouds, above the seas, in

your home,

illuminating their dominions.

(posted June 26th 2010 translated Jack Schmitt re-formatted M.Stow)

Also by M.Stow:

Walter Mepham (A First World War true family and personal stories)

EarthCentre: The End of the Universe (An Anthropic Odyssey)

Universal Verses

Arctol Continuum

Pan Tan-Gou Paradise Won!

WarFair4 part two: The Day The Market's Collapsed

WarFair4 part three: The Day The Market's Finally Collapsed

PHW Young British Artist 1970's London&Paris: The Lot.

paul howard williams video art gallery 2019 youtube

WF4.225.

Paul Howard Williams Artwork:

Young British Artist 1970`s London & Paris: The Lot

WF4.226.

WF4.227.

Printed in Great Britain
by Amazon